In Love with
a Brooklyn Thug

In Love with a Brooklyn Thug

Nako

www.urbanbooks.net

Urban Books, LLC
300 Farmingdale Road, NY-Route 109
Farmingdale, NY 11735

ISBN 13: 978-1-945855-42-9
ISBN 10: 1-945855-42-8

First Trade Paperback Printing September 2018
Printed in the United States of America

10 9 8 7 6 5 4 3 2 1

Distributed by Kensington Publishing Corp.
Submit Orders to:
Customer Service
400 Hahn Road
Westminster, MD 21157-4627
Phone: 1-800-733-3000
Fax: 1-800-659-2436

In Love with a Brooklyn Thug

by

Nako

Write about love. My favorite thing to do.
I was created for this.

From my heart to yours,

—Nako

Chanique, thank you for the inspiration. From one post on Facebook, my eighteenth book was created. No outline, no deadline, and no notes.

Just love, music, a semi-broken heart, my laptop, and me.

God bless you, girlie.

1

"I know they say the first love is the sweetest, but that
first cut is the deepest."

— Drake

"Really? You gon' stand there like you don't see dude
looking at you?" Porsche asked her cousin.

Nia rolled her eyes and popped her gum. She did not
go to anyone. If homeboy wanted her digits, he needed
to make his tall ass go over to her and get 'em. Hollering
across a crowded parking lot wasn't the way to capture
her attention. The Summer Jam concert had just ended,
and people were flooding the streets, trying to get to their
cars. Nia was hot, tired, and sweaty, and her voice was
gone from screaming at the top of her lungs when her
favorite rapper, Jay-Z, hit the stage.

"Girl, I'm not stunting that man, and you shouldn't be,
either. Let's go," Nia spat, ready to catch the train and
head back home.

"Yo, you're so wack sometimes," her cousin complained.

Nia ignored her, pulled her long hair into a bun, and
tied it with the rubber band that she kept on her wrist for
temperatures like this. Summertime on Long Island was
sticky and humid, and she was anticipating sitting buck
naked in the air-conditioning once she made it back to
Brooklyn.

"Ayo, sweetie," said a voice from behind her.

Being that her name wasn't sweetie, Nia kept walking, not bothered by the catcall.

"Whoa. Hold on, Mama. Just give me a second," insisted the voice, closer now.

But she refused to stop her stroll. A touch on her shoulder brought a scowl to her face, and instantly, her fist balled up. Nia spun around on her heels, ready to go the fuck off if need be.

"Don't touch . . . ," she warned before she was rendered speechless.

Never had that happened before. Nia wasn't easily impressed by the men who approached her. She had been that way for about two years now. The death of a past lover had her mentally stagnant and physically unavailable. She was not in the mood to share her time or her bed with the opposite sex.

"You been ignoring me all day," he said with a smile.

"All day? You clearly got the wrong one," she told him, assuming that he had her confused with another chick, although she knew no one looked like her or *was* her, for that matter.

She was well aware that she was a rare gem and was in a league all her own. Nia did not compete when she knew others just did not compare.

"Nah, you are the right one. I can't forget those hips at all," he said, licking his lips and admiring the brown goddess from head to toe.

She looked down and shifted her stance, appearing to be uncomfortable. No one had made her speechless in quite a while, and she was unaware of how to handle this situation. As she looked down, she stared at her fat, short toes in the Gucci sandals she had decided to wear today.

"What you looking down for? I'm up here," he said. The way she had bucked just a minute ago had him hesitant to touch her face and lift her chin.

"Girl, come on, before we miss the train," her cousin said, rushing her.

Nia turned her head and smirked in Porsche's direction. It was funny how when she was not paying the gentlemen no attention, her cousin called her wack and corny and a bore, but to see a dude all in her personal space had Porsche tight.

The absurdity of some women.

"Give me a second," she told Porsche, holding up a manicured finger to signify that she needed some time, since the redbone cutie now had her attention, and her attention was not something that everyone wasn't liable to capture. But for some reason, he had.

He smiled and offered his name. "East," he told her.

Nia raised an eyebrow and bit on her bottom lip. "East? That's your real name?" she asked, never have heard this name before.

He nodded his head, pulled his vibrating phone out of his pocket, and looked at it for a few seconds. "Damn, Ma. I gotta slide, but I want to get to know you," he said. His voice held so much persistence.

She knew her heart was not capable of loving him. She couldn't . . . not right now . . . not after *him*. Nia shook her head. "If it's meant to be, you'll see me around," she told him, knowing that it was time for her to move on.

He sighed, but East wasn't one to press a woman. As beautiful as she was, and as melodic as her voice was to his ears, he would not chase her. He believed in God aligning things in his favor, so in due time. . . .

"You take care of yourself," he told her, meaning every single word.

Before Nia could repeat the words back to him, her loud and obnoxious cousin was screaming for her to come along.

Nia blew out a breath of frustration. "You too," she mumbled, and then she stomped off.

Porsche rolled her eyes once Nia had finally caught up with her.

"Girl, you wasn't even stunting him at first," she said, attempting to crack a joke, but Nia didn't find anything funny.

Nia barely offered two words to her cousin as they traveled back home. Once they walked through the door, Nia walked down the steps to the basement, her safe haven, and locked the door to what she called her bedroom. It wasn't much, but it was comfortable, and she made do with what she had.

She stripped off her clothes went into her bathroom, and hopped in the shower, but she did not stay in too long, because she did not want to hear her auntie's mouth. Nia hated spending the summers at her aunt's, and she was desperately counting down the days until it was time for her to return to school. She had two years of college to go and had yet to land an internship or even a possible job opportunity, but she was keeping the faith. Nia refused to give up on her dream of becoming a world-renowned fashion designer, and she was well aware of her potential. She just needed someone else to see it as well.

Instead of majoring in fashion merchandising or design, as Google had suggested, she had majored in business management, with a minor in marketing, which was more realistic for her. She was about her coins, and although she spent countless hours watching YouTube videos on designing clothes, it came naturally to her. She planned to land a job in corporate America to fund her dreams. Nia was a practical person, with a heart made of gold.

After her ten-minute shower, and not a minute after—since she set her alarm to alert her to get out at a certain time—she threw on a pair of leggings and a shirt and grabbed her sketchbook, preparing to draw a few designs, since she was inspired at Summer Jam.

The large sketchbook was tattered at the edges, but she refused to buy another one. It seemed as if the pages were endless. Nia had other sketchbooks, but this one held the magic. Anything she sketched in this one particular book always looked runway ready. She knew that it was only her being dramatic, since this sketchbook was a gift, and it was the last gift she'd received from *him*.

Nia pushed her back against the wall, and with her headphones on, she cracked her neck and got to work. Countless hours passed, and the young girl didn't even know she had fallen asleep until there was a knock at the door. When she opened her eyes, the sun was blazing into her room, signifying that another day had come.

"Yes?" she said kindly to the person who was on the other side of the door, banging as if they had no sense.

"Walk to the corner store with me. Ma is out of eggs," Porsche told her, since she damn sure didn't ask.

Nia rolled her eyes, wondering why her cousin couldn't go by herself. If Nia were away at school, her cousin would have to go alone, but she agreed to go, wanting to keep the peace. "Give me ten minutes," she told her, yawning and peeling herself from the bed.

She closed her sketchbook and slid it under her pillow. Nia went into her bathroom, brushed her teeth, and washed her face, skipping her daily routine of exfoliating her oily skin.

"I need to pick up some more black soap," she said to herself.

Growing up with a face full of acne used to be the worst thing to a teenager, but with water and black soap, her face was looking good. She just knew she had to keep it up.

Nia smiled at her appearance in the mirror. Learning to love herself was one of the hardest things she had had to do. Even now, it was still a struggle, and she had to accept that she still had a few insecurities, but some progress was better than none. After losing her high school sweetheart to gun violence, she had had no choice but to pick herself up, put her life back together, and somehow find happiness again. However, since the pieces were made of him, it had been easier said than done. Biggs had been her everything: her love, her life, her best friend, her daddy, and her protector. Losing him had been the worst day of her life. She had not even cried that hard at her own mother's funeral. Nia loved him more than anything else in this world. In a weird way, she knew that everything had happened for a reason. She had had no plans of attending college or making a living for herself while she was dating a man like Biggs.

His name matched him perfectly, she thought as she imagined a seventeen-year-old girl madly in love with the biggest dope dealer in the hood. And he had loved her back. Wholeheartedly.

Nia had been the apple of his eye, and everyone had known it too. His death had not been a surprise. Sadly, with the life that he had lived and the snakes in his circle, it had almost been expected. However, not for Nia. She could not believe it.

She was a brand-new person these days. She didn't have the riches any more, but she had her happiness, and that alone made her content. She had enrolled in college and had received a scholarship since her grades were decent while she was in high school. No, she hadn't done things like everyone else, and she had not felt bad about being a twenty-one-year-old freshman in college, either. She had known then that she had to get her money, and college had been the only route she was willing to take.

She needed to keep money in her pocket while she was in college. The girl was too damn pretty for prison, so busting checks and robbing were not her thing. Nia wasn't prone to popping her pussy for strange men, so she couldn't strip or turn tricks. She didn't like standing on her feet or dealing with too many different attitudes, so that axed out every other job in America. Her only option was to put her pastime to use, and that was what she did to make some money. Nia made clothes, dyed jeans, and customized phone cases, sneakers, and even wineglasses. It was enough business to keep her cell phone bill paid and to keep food in her apartment. Besides that, her only other concerns were her hair, nails, and feet, typical girl things. She was not a bopper, barely having left the house to socialize since her man died. Nia was focused on her books and on landing a good job. After college, moving back into her aunt's basement would not be an option for her. No matter what circumstances and trials she would have to face, she refused to live with that woman and her daughter.

She had raised herself, since the woman who had blessed her with life wasn't suitable to be a mother. She was the only child and didn't exactly know who her father was, but according to some rumors she had heard, he was a petty thief. On other occasions she had heard that her mother had met some man in Atlantic City and had come back knocked up.

Nia believed she had clung to Biggs the way she had because she had always been searching for love and validation.

Nia slid her feet into a pair of worn Air Max tennis shoes and headed to the stairs, expecting to find her cousin upstairs, but Porsche was chilling on Nia's couch in the basement.

"That's what you wearing?" her cousin asked, with disgust in her voice.

Nia looked down at the clothes she had on and wondered what the problem was if they were only going around the corner to the store. "Um, yeah," she said slowly.

"Always dress like you're about to meet your husband," Porsche declared, thinking she was schooling her cousin, as she stood to her feet and combed her fingers through her pressed weave.

Nia chuckled and kept her comment to herself. *Girl, fuck a husband. I am trying to meet a check.*

She and Porsche were on two different levels in life, and for that reason, she remained at school throughout the semester and hardly came to her aunt's house. She did not consider the place home at all.

They walked to the corner store in silence. Nia was wrapped up in her thoughts, and Porsche was busy trying to take in the neighborhood in hopes of capturing someone's attention.

"Li'l Nia," someone hollered from across the street.

With her hand hovering near her forehead to block the sun, Nia tried to get a better glimpse at the person who had called her name and had added a "li'l" in front it, knowing that Biggs was the only person who called her that. She squinted one of her eyes to get a better look and saw that it was Harlem, Biggs's cousin. A smile crept across her face.

Nia turned around, told her cousin, "I'll be back. You can run in the store without me." And then she crossed the street, not waiting on Porsche to respond.

She didn't need anyone with her all the time. If she had learned anything from her past lover's death, it was to be independent.

"Oh my God. It's been so long," she said as she greeted Harlem with a hug.

He said, "Look at you, kid. Still fly."

Nia thought about her cousin's weak attempt at an insult just a few minutes before and laughed inwardly. She never had to try too hard to look cute.

"I threw this on," she said, waving him off.

Harlem took in all of Nia's appearance. She was different, not like the other girls around here, and his cousin had known that.

"Yo, you good? You need anything? You know I don't be around these parts too often," he said.

Everyone still showed love to Nia whenever she decided to grace places with her face. Biggs had been well respected in every borough in New York, and even in a few places down South.

She shook her head. Although she could use an extra few hundred dollars to buy supplies, she would not dare fix her lips to ask for anything, especially with all these niggas around.

"You sure?" he asked, sensing the hesitance in her demeanor.

"Yep. It was good seeing you, Harlem. Stay safe," she told him.

He nodded his head. "Always, Ma."

She turned and walked down the block to cross the street, since there were a few cars rolling through.

He called her name again, then slowly jogged toward her. Before she could say anything, he slid a bankroll in her hand and kissed her on the forehead. "Be good, youngin'."

She looked down at the money, all hundred-dollar bills, from what she could see. "Thank you," were the only two words she could muster.

Across the street, her cousin Porsche watched on, overtaken by envy, as one of the heaviest niggas in the city gawked at Nia. What she didn't know was that Harlem would not dare step to his cousin's girl. Although Biggs was no longer here, that was not how Harlem rolled, and he knew if the shoe was on the other foot, his cousin would do the same.

"How much money did that dude give you?" Porsche asked her hours and hours later.

Nia wasn't sure if she had heard her cousin correctly, so she didn't say anything, just continued to eat dinner in silence.

"Nia." Porsche waved her long fingernails in front of her cousin's face.

Nia sat back in her seat and shot her cousin an evil glare. "Don't put your hand in my face no more," she warned.

Porsche cackled. "Well, damn, bitch. You act like you don't hear me."

"You asked me about some money, right?" Nia questioned.

Porsche nodded her head. "Uh, yeah. I saw that fine-ass nigga trying to trick off on you," she told her.

Nia smirked. "Is that what it's called when someone looks out? Oh, I didn't know."

Her cousin continued. "I'm just saying, you wasn't even going to come to the store at first."

Now Nia was confused. "And so what?" she asked, wanting to know what the hell Porsche was getting at with all this nonsense.

"And so what? Bitch, you live here rent free. Your selfish ass did not even try to say, 'Here you go, cuz,' or give my mama nothing," Porsche snapped. "We do not say anything when you sit your li'l pretty ass in the tub and use all the hot water, or when you are up in all our good groceries. And then you be having all kinds of hoes over here, ordering clothes, but not once did you offer to make me anything."

Nia sat in silence for a few moments, processing every single word her cousin had said to her. She took it all in, and then she took one last bite of the rice and cabbage mixture that she had put together before getting out of the chair and going to the basement, where she made sure to lock the bedroom door.

She hummed quietly as she grabbed the essentials and an overnight bag and packed up as much as she could, having decided that everything else could be replaced. She walked back up the steps to find Porsche whispering to her mother, Nia's aunt.

Nia slapped the bankroll on the table and said, "I don't even need this money." And then she walked around them and headed to the door.

"Girl, where is your ass going? You ain't got any family here. Go back in that basement and cool out. You and Porsche gotta stop acting like that," her aunt fussed.

No, your daughter needs to stop being a hater.

She had no words for the only family she had left in this world, and those two together weren't much of nothing to brag about. Nia called a cab, left, and stayed in a hotel room until the morning came. The next day she took a train back to school, where she got lucky, landed a summer job, and never looked back.

She told herself that she had to succeed by any means necessary, because all she had was herself. She had no Mama, no Daddy, no known siblings, no real or supportive extended family, only minor friends, and a nigga who was gone.

Nia hustled; she hustled as if her last meal depended on it.

A few years later, it all paid off.

2

"You let me call the shots, my vision is SO VIVID, and you allowed me to show it to the world and I thank you."

– Chloe Claire

"Shit," Nia moaned out in pure satisfaction after she finally reached her peak, the lava in her volcano pouring out of her and all over the leather chair she sat in, with her satin panties and Burberry print trousers around her ankles.

That "in the middle of the day" nut was the business. She loved it. Before a meeting and after a conference call, she seemed to squeeze them in a few times in the week. She slowly caught her breath and wiped away a little sweat that had begun to form on her forehead. Nia smiled and bit her bottom lip, as if the man of her dreams had blessed her with the best head she had ever received. Instead, her little magic bullet had done the trick. After wiping the vibrator off with a Kleenex, she tossed it back into the drawer, under a few contracts and files, and then pulled her panties and pants up, buckled her belt, and slid her feet back into her red bottoms.

It had been quite a while since she had given her body to a man, and even longer since she had offered her heart in return for love. The time or the person simply had not presented itself to her, so instead she worked. Nia worked so damn hard. It was the sacrifice she was willing to make to get where she truly desired to be. The ringing phone on her work desk made her jump, but she answered it on the third ring.

"Nia Hudson," she answered, knowing that it was the receptionist at the front of the building she now owned.

"Ms. Hudson, the editor from *Vogue* is on the other line. She is asking if you have received the final draft of the article before it goes to print," the woman said.

Nia scanned her memory and realized that right before she started toying with her insides, she had checked her e-mail.

"No. But let me check again. One second," she told the receptionist.

She sat back down at her desk, and with one swipe of her finger, her Mac computer came back to life. She refreshed her e-mail and saw three new and unread e-mails.

"Got it. Tell her I will read it before sending it to Amy. The end of the day is when she should expect an e-mail from me," she said.

"Will do. And for lunch, do you need me to order anything?" her receptionist said kindly.

Nia smiled. See, this was why she loved her team. Kate was not responsible for making sure Nia ate, but her assistant was away on maternity leave, and she would not dare hire another in her absence. Therefore, everyone had begun to take up the slack and help out around the office, even if it was not in their contract, in the description of the job requirements.

"No thank you. I brought lunch with me today," Nia told her, thinking of the leftover lasagna she had in the fridge under her desk.

"Okay. Sounds good," Kate said cheerfully.

Nia ended the call, put the phone back on the cradle, and opened the e-mail from the *Vogue* editor. She could not help but feel giddy on the inside. Staring up at the ceiling, as if she could see the sky, she smiled. Biggs would be so proud of her. He had believed in her. He had told her that she possessed the power to be anything she wanted to be. Nia had struggled with finding her footing her whole life. She hadn't been able to identify her purpose, and after starting several businesses and failing, she had considered giving up and going to get a job. However, that had not been what she wanted, and the whole time she'd known that she had it in her.

Nia read aloud the headline for the article, which was set to be in next month's issue. "Nia Hudson, multimillionaire, shares her story of the downfalls of success and tells how tackling your fears can lead you to the top of the competitive fashion industry."

Nia was transparent in the article. She rarely shared her downfalls or her horror stories of raising herself, losing the love of her life, and starting college three years after graduating high school, but she did for the article. She even talked about how at one point, she was down to her last thousand dollars and spent it on materials to continue to fund her dreams. On her lunch break at different dead-end jobs, she would sew clothes for clients. She called it working at work. Nia was about her money and her dreams, too, but nothing seemed to come together for her.

After graduation, she slowly gave up on her vision of becoming a fashion designer and settled on a job that kept the lights on. She was lost and did not have a clue what her next direction was. One day a classmate from college dialed her number, praying that it was still the same. Nia answered, not recognizing the number, and wondered who was calling her. That call changed her life. Her classmate was the youngest daughter of Morris Favors, one of the greatest singers of all time. She was in panic mode as she needed a dress for an award ceremony she was going to with her family. Nia told her that she didn't do sewing anymore, but the desperation in her classmate's voice caused her to pull out her old trusty sewing machine and get to work.

Surprisingly, the dress was the talk of the night, and from there Nia's life changed. One client became ten, ten turned into forty, and before she knew it, she was purchasing a design studio. She never lived outside of her means, having learned that from Biggs. It took Nia awhile to upgrade her lifestyle, but it felt so good to purchase her first car and home with cash. Nia went from a one-woman army to a three-person team to transitioning into a mogul.

At the tender age of twenty-eight, she was now a household name and a pillar in the community. She had been featured in several different magazines, on television shows, and on Web sites. Clients had become friends, and a few of those friends had turned into women whom she called her sisters. Nia lived in Manhattan and loved being in the city, but she also traveled often. She turned up with her team when time permitted.

Nia was now the proud owner of ND Studios, a three-story building where she made clothes for the slim and thick, the curvy, and the tall women too. She catered to every figure. The third floor was where her seamstresses were located, and contrary to popular belief, Nia still did this kind of work. She designed pretty much anything a client requested, but her first love had been dresses, so it wasn't surprising that she found her niche in wedding dresses. The process of bringing a bride's vision to life for her special day was one of Nia's favorite things to do. When a bride paid her to create a wedding dress, she designed it and sewed it herself.

The first floor of the building was an exclusive boutique that opened only on Saturdays. The pieces included in the store were rare, and Nia produced only three of each. The second floor of the building was where the suites were located. She ran a profitable business with a team of ten. Nia knew that she couldn't do it alone, nor did she try to anymore. She had also started her own business blog, and she often spoke at colleges and universities in hopes of encouraging students not to give up on their dreams.

After making sure the article was up to her standard, she forwarded the e-mail to her publicist so she could handle the rest. Mondays were her favorite days because they set the tone for the rest of the week. Nia had a long, productive day ahead of her, and she was looking forward to it. And her work would continue after office hours today. She had plans to catch an aspiring designer's fashion show tonight with two of her girlfriends, Samone and Nasi.

She was about to get up to ask Kate about ordering a bouquet of roses for the designer whose fashion show she was attending tonight when she remembered she had two other e-mails. After pressing the BACK button on her browser, she saw the simple subject message, which read, "I know you don't know me but . . ." It piqued her interest, and Nia opened the e-mail immediately. There were not too many people who had her e-mail, and her personal one at that. On her Web site, messages in the suggestion and comment box went directly to her publicist and business manager. Nia sat back in her seat and read the e-mail twice, in awe at the nerve of this woman. She shook her head and closed the browser and went to check on her staff.

During the fashion show, Nia's attention span was as short as that of a three-year-old sitting in church on

Easter Sunday. She could not concentrate at all and found herself rereading the unnerving e-mail multiple times.

Nasi, her best friend, teased, "Let me find out someone sending you love notes."

Nia mumbled, "Hell, I wish."

She sighed and slid her phone into her Chanel purse and redirected her focus to the fashion show. This was the one day she regretted having front-row seats. She did not want to appear to be uninterested, knowing how it felt to be behind the curtain, to stare out at the crowd, and to see several designers in the position you desired to be in looking bored and ready to go. She sat up and crossed one foot behind the other and paid attention.

After the show, she went backstage to congratulate the young woman on a job well done and to wish her the best. The woman, whose name was Chelle, was so full of joy at seeing Nia Hudson.

"You really came? Oh my God, thank you," she said repeatedly. She smiled and gave Nia a warm hug. Then she turned and said, "Babe, take this picture for me."

When the guy turned around, Nia was not expecting to see *him*.

"Harlem, what are you doing here?" she asked.

The chick, Chelle, was no longer smiling. "Y'all know each other?"

They both ignored her, and Harlem gave Nia a big hug.

"Girl, I heard about you. Didn't expect to see you here, though," he told her.

Nia said, "Wow. It's been so long. Like what? Five years?"

It was so good to see a familiar face. After she left her aunt's house, she'd barely kept in touch, and when she graduated, she had not even bothered sending an invitation. Nia had gone to college for herself . . . and Biggs too. She had not needed anyone at her commencement who wasn't genuinely happy for her.

"Sounds about right," he said, then paused. "Yo, this is my girl. Babe, this is my family," Harlem added, finally introducing the two women.

Chelle could not believe Harlem knew someone on such a high pedestal. Nia Hudson was the shit in the fashion industry. She was considered a *gawd* of the runways. Teenagers, young women, and even the forty-and-over crew looked up to her and admired her style. Nia could post a picture of herself snuggled up on the couch, reading a book, and instantly, people would rush to Amazon and buy the book. That was how strong her following was.

But Nia was a simple chick who had not forgotten the past. For instance, she still checked her bank accounts daily, like they were in overdraft. She would never forget the bad days, because they made her appreciate the good days. She was a very humble woman.

"You . . . you know her?" Chelle could not even keep her cool anymore.

Harlem and Nia shared a laugh, because they both knew where Nia came from, and it was straight out of the projects.

"Girl, yeah. I used to pick li'l Nia up from school and drop her off at the hair salon," he said.

Nia remembered the good ole days as if they were yesterday. She knew Biggs was looking down and smiling at her right now.

"What you doing tonight? Come out with us. We celebrating," Harlem insisted.

She shook her head. Every now and then Nia would go out and turn up, but tonight wasn't one of those nights. *A Monday night? No, sir*, she thought.

"I wish I had the energy, but I don't, and I got my girls with me," she said, motioning to the curtain. They were probably behind it, circling the crowd, networking.

Samone was the hottest tattoo artist up North, and Nasi was the girlfriend of Harry Cromwell, point guard for the New York Knicks. Prior to linking up with him, she had a popular bakery, but these days she baked only for her man and her girls when their sweet tooth needed satisfying.

"They can come too. You know it's all love," Harlem said.

She saw the look in his eyes and knew that he hadn't changed. He was still a ladies' man.

"Give me your number. I'll see what they're talking about," Nia told him.

It was not like she had anything urgent to do tomorrow. Nia worked for herself. She made her schedule, but for the most part, she woke up early every day, went to her office Monday through Friday, and worked her boutique on Saturdays.

She chose to have her boutique open for only one day each week for a very specific reason. It kept her store exclusive, and for that reason, people would anticipate the weekend. In addition, every month the styles were switched, and this also kept people coming back. The way her brand was set up was perfect, and every day she was researching new ways to make it better.

"All right now. Call me," he told her.

She smiled and promised to hit him up if her girls decided to step out. She took a few pictures and decided that since she was friends with Harlem, she would post a selfie on her Instagram. She knew that her 2.3 million followers would go follow her.

"Y'all heffas ready to go?" she asked her friends when she caught up with them.

"Girl, Khloe said to meet her at EVOL tonight, and I think Harry is going to be there, so you know I want to go," Nasi said.

Samone jumped in. "Of course you want to. Y'all live together, and he takes good care of you. Baby girl, you ain't got shit to worry about," she told Nasi for the millionth time.

Nia never said anything. She knew how it felt to date a man with money and power and to question your position. Been there, done that before.

"Oh, shut up. We are still going," Nasi insisted and waved her off.

"Can I wear what I got on?" Nia asked Nasi. "I never been to EVOL, and I don't feel like changing." She wore a yellow blazer on top of a white screen tee that read BOOKS OVER BOYS. She was an avid reader, and she loved T-shirts. Her denim jeans hugged her thick hips and voluptuous thighs perfectly, and they went well with the Givenchy pumps. The outfit was perfect, and she didn't have to change at all.

"Yeah, you good if you take that country fish braid out of your hair," Samone said and laughed.

Nia stuck her tongue out. "Whatever. Let's go eat. I'm starving," she told them.

After indulging in sushi and wine, the trio caught an Uber to the club since Khloe had texted Nasi and had said the valet parking lot was full.

"Are our cars safe there?" Samone asked, not comfortable leaving her Range Rover in an almost empty parking lot.

"Well, do you want to take yours to my condo?" Nia asked her friend.

"Girl, we are ten minutes away from the club now," Nasi fussed.

Nia was staring into a compact mirror, reapplying a fresh coat of YSL lipstick. "I think they're going to be okay," she announced, but Samone wasn't relaxed.

"I might not stay long, y'all," she told them.

Nia did not plan to be out all night, either. She was looking forward to taking a hot bath and reading a book until she fell asleep. There were a few things on her mind she needed to process, like the e-mail she'd received earlier today.

Of course, they didn't have to stand in line or wait at the bar once they arrived at the club. The women followed Nasi into the section that their mutual friend Khloe had rented out. Then they got their drinks.

The music was jamming, and the apple martini Nia was sipping on was good and strong. She saw Harlem and Chelle, the fashion designer, walking through the door, and so everything had worked out in her favor. Now she didn't have to feel bad tomorrow for skipping out on them.

Nia told Samone that she was coming right back and went to speak to Harlem and Chelle and show her face.

"Aye, you came! How you know we were gone be here?" Chelle said when Nia appeared in front of her.

Before Nia could tell her that she hadn't known, she saw Biggs's little brother, Boscey. "Boscey, is that you?" she asked and stood on her tippy toes to touch his shoulder.

Boscey was not a little boy anymore. The tall man standing before her had grown up, and apparently, he was in these streets, as he reached for his gun but then stopped once he saw it was Nia.

"Nia, *damn*. Nia-Nia, what it do, Ma?" he said. His voice wasn't light and squeaky anymore.

They hugged for what seemed longer than two minutes. When they separated, Nia didn't realize her eyes had become misty until Chelle handed her a napkin that she had under her cup.

"Ooh, don't judge me," Nia told them.

Harlem, Boscey, and the few other people with them understood exactly how she felt. Being around familiar faces brought back memories, and Boscey smelled just like Biggs. Gosh, she'd missed him so much.

Nia struggled with her next sentence, trying to control her emotions. "How have you been?" she asked him kindly.

Boscey looked down, as if he was almost disappointed, then said, "Grinding, Nia."

She hated that this life had chosen him, since she knew he hadn't willingly chosen it, especially not after the way his big brother was murdered.

"You be safe out here. Harlem, keep him near you," Nia yelled over the music.

"Now, you know my nigga wouldn't have us doing things any other way," Boscey told her, referring to Biggs.

"Yep, he wouldn't," she said after taking a deep breath. "Damn, Boscey. You done grew up," she told him, still not believing it.

"Mama is always talking about you. You should call her," he said.

Nia knew that Boscey was telling the truth, but being around all of them would only dampen her spirits. Although years had passed since Biggs's death, she still had not really let him go.

"I will," she told him, half telling the truth.

"I follow you on Instagram too. Follow me back," he said, then laughed, lightening up the conversation.

Nia pulled her phone out of the back pocket of her jeans. "Honey, type your name in," she told him as she handed him the phone.

She eyed the other folks who were with them, looking for any familiar faces, but she saw none. One of the guys caught her staring, and she did a double take but decided she'd never seen him before. Then she turned her attention back to Boscey.

"Okay, little bro, I got you. I am going to send you my number," she said as he handed her back her phone. "How often are you in Manhattan?" she asked, knowing he probably still kicked it in the hood.

He shrugged his shoulders. "I'm up here with Harlem. This ain't even my speed, know what I mean?" he told her.

"Well, whenever you here, call me," she told him.

"Okay, Nia." He side hugged her once more, and she told Harlem she was going back over to her friends.

She returned to Khloe's section and resumed the turn up with her homegirls, unaware that so many eyes were on her. It was not only because she was considered a celebrity, but because she was just as beautiful in person as she was on social media, and she appeared not to have a care in the world, though the truth was that her heart and soul were empty.

Unlike her friends, who had people to go home to tonight, she would be returning to a cold condo and getting into bed with herself. Nia had it all, supposedly—a great life and a successful, thriving career. She had an awesome team and amazing friends, and even her passport had lots of stamps, but she was not complete. She wanted love. Biggs's love would be great, but she knew that was not possible. It pained her that he didn't visit her as often as he used to in her dreams.

In a weird way, Nia felt as if he was pushing her to move on, to live, and to find love.

On the other side of the club, East asked Harlem, "What was her name?"

Harlem sipped the Henn and eyed his best friend. "Who?" He was playing games, since he knew damn well whom East was talking about.

"Shorty in the yellow," East told him.

Harlem shook his head. "My man's girl," he informed him, hoping he would drop the conversation.

"Your man's who, nigga?" East asked, knowing everyone Harlem hung with, which was with no one but him.

The other people with them were what East referred to as TTG Squad. They were gremlins who were trained to go and would not hesitate to shoot at all.

Harlem said, "Yo, my brother. I love you like my mama pushed you out, and that's my word, but not her, man, not her."

East wasn't hearing anything he was saying. One, the club was loud, and Harlem's voice was low and raspy, on top of him being high and tipsy; and two, East was a grown-ass man and made his own decisions. East knew that Harlem always had his best interests at heart, but he planned to pursue the cutie. She looked too good and too familiar not to. There was something about her that he remembered, but with the amount of weed he had consumed today, he could not place a finger on it.

However, that smile, those eyes, her lips and hips . . . He knew that tonight wasn't the first time he'd seen her.

The night progressed, and East bobbed to the tunes of a few of the greats. The night was still young when he realized he was tired. He hadn't kept count of how many times he had yawned in the past thirty minutes, but he decided that it was enough and that it was time for him to haul his ass home. East could not hang as much as he used to.

Across the crowded club, in six-inch heels, Nia was feeling the exact same way as East. Samone had caught a cab to her truck two hours ago, and Nasi was somewhere running behind her man. Nia shot her a text telling her to be safe, and with that, she was out the side door in less than five minutes. She knew that she should not be going out any side doors, but the route through the club was crowded and her feet were aching, so she chose the easiest way out.

"Do you know where you are, miss?" said a voice in front of her. It was so dark, she could not see to whom it belonged.

It scared the shit out of her.

She screamed and flapped her arms up and down. "Oh my God!"

East backed up and held his hands up. "Didn't mean to startle you," he said, apologizing.

She rolled her eyes and said, "Don't do that."

After letting out a light chuckle, he asked, "What are you gon' do?"

Nia found nothing funny. Every day innocent women were being mugged, kidnapped, raped and, even worse, killed. She now regretted being lazy and running out the first door she'd spotted.

"Kill your ass," she mumbled and kept walking, keeping her hand on her purse.

As nicely dressed as the man was, she did not put anything past anyone. There were so many people posing as others these days. Normally, the ones who were flashy had the lightest pockets.

East watched her walk past him and could not help but to take in her appearance. She was so fly, and even after a few drinks, she was still composed.

He called out to her, not wanting to miss the opportunity. "I think I know you," he said.

She blew air out of her mouth, frustrated, feet hurting, and not in the mood to be dealing with bullshit or foolery.

"I've heard that before," she told him and kept walking.

East knew he wasn't drunk or tripping out. "Nah, nah, like, know you. Maybe I saw you at a game or something," he said, trying to rack his brain.

Nia rolled her eyes and turned down the block, not remembering that her car wasn't in the parking lot. She could not believe this fool was following her. His cologne invaded her nostrils, and she was secretly happy he was near, in case another crazy came to harm her. He would protect her, hopefully.

"You don't know me, man, and I don't know you," she told him seriously.

East ran his hand over his beard. "Damn. I know I'm not tripping. Okay, what about, um . . . Summer Jam? Fucking right. Summer Jam. You were at Summer Jam with a girl," he said loudly.

Good thing it was four in the morning and no one was really wandering the streets. Nia knew what he was talking about, because it was around that time that she had left her aunt's house and had started grinding like never before.

She stopped mid stroll. "You were trying to get my number in the parking lot?" she asked.

He smiled, showing off his perfectly aligned teeth. "Yeah, something like that, but you were brushing me off at first. I see some things haven't changed," he told her.

Nia said, "Yeah, that hasn't changed. I still curve 'em."

East respected that. At least he knew she wasn't giving it up to everybody round here.

"I like that, though. Makes me chase you," he told her, licking his bottom lip, but not on purpose.

She looked away, not enjoying the feeling he was giving her, which was a feeling of bliss.

"Where is your car? At least let me get you there safe," he suggested once she went silent and kept on walking.

She smacked her lips. "Damn, man," she said angrily.

"What's wrong?" East questioned, not wanting his future boo to be mad.

"My car . . . It's at Ra. I caught an Uber." She stomped her feet.

He could tell she was spoiled, but he did not know that she had been spoiling herself for almost eight years now.

"Which one?" he asked.

"Thirteenth Street. But it's okay. My homegirl is in there. I'll just ask her boyfriend to take me home," she said, not wanting to go back in the club.

"I can take you to your car," East told her.

Nia raised an eyebrow and told him, "Uh, no, sir. I like my life."

He was taken back. "And I like my freedom," he told her.

"You don't know me, and I don't know you," she reminded him.

East begged to differ. "Well, technically, we do know each other, boo." He smiled.

Nia was not smiling. She was sleepy, and her feet hurt.

"Thank you, but no thank you," she told him before she turned around and walked in the direction of the club.

East grabbed her hand gently, not wanting to tick her off any more than he already had.

"I'm cool with your people Harlem. I wouldn't let anything happen to you," he said, trying again. He knew there had to be something about her, because this wasn't how he operated at all.

Nia was about to tell him she did not give a damn if he knew Brooklyn and Queens, but she didn't. She pointed her finger in his direction. "I will have some niggas come see about you if you do something to me," she threatened.

East had no idea who Harlem had been referring to when he told him that she was off limits, and East really did not give a fuck. He had given his loyalty to Harlem, but it did not extend on down to the people he knew and rocked with. East was his own man. He went for what he wanted, and right now that was shorty.

"Girl, please. Come on," he said, and she slowly but surely followed him to a white Mercedes-Benz coupe.

She hadn't even seen the inside of this car yet, but damn, it had her speechless.

"I like this," she told him once she had her seat belt on and he was pulling out of the parking lot. But he was not going fast enough.

Harlem, Chelle, Boscey, and the crew spotted East as he sped in front of the club, stopped at the red light, and then accelerated when it turned green.

"Who that in the car with East?" one of the dudes asked no one in particular.

"Shit. Ain't no telling," another dude said.

Harlem hoped it wasn't li'l Nia.

"You drive really fast," Nia commented minutes later.

East turned the air down. "Oh, you can't handle speed?" he asked.

She felt as if he wasn't referring only to how he drove his car, so she said nothing.

"Make a right up here," she instructed a few minutes later.

East pulled his car into the parking lot, and only her car was parked there.

"This you?" he asked, liking the black Audi.

"Yep, this is me." She nodded her head. "Thank you so much."

East told her, "It's nothing. Anything for you." He was too smooth for her.

"Well, all right. Get home safe, or wherever you're headed," she said, but she made no move to get out of his car.

"Home. To think about you," he said.

She smiled. "You're too much," she admitted.

"That's what you probably need, Ms. Bossy," he teased.

"Can't argue with you there," Nia said, knowing that she tended to turn into a bitch, especially when it was time to release a new line or prepare for a fashion show.

She was a perfectionist and did not apologize for it.

"East, in case you forgot," he reminded her.

Nia held her hand out. "Nia, in case I didn't even tell you," she joked.

He laughed a little. "Pleasure to meet you."

She replied, "Again," and winked.

"When can I see you?" East asked her, pressing.

Nia went to give him her famous "I'm really focused right now" line, but it did not come out. In fact, she had nothing to say.

East stared at her, waiting on her to say something, wondering whether she would agree to see him or would turn him down. She looked like she had blanked out.

"Yo, Ma? You good?" he asked.

She closed her open mouth and said, "Um, yeah, I'm good. Sorry. I'm tired."

"We can do lunch tomorrow. How about that? I'll take things slow," he told her.

Nia stared at his bottom lip. *Heavenly*, she thought to herself.

She responded slowly. "Okay."

East smiled. He seemed to have that effect on the ladies, but he hadn't expected to have Nia mesmerized as well.

Knowing that he was sexy did not help, either. Hailing from Brooklyn, he was a certified thug. His skin was the color of melted butter pecan ice cream; his eyes were the color of a rotten apple, with speckles of honeydew. He was tall in stature, standing at six feet four even. He had waves that would cause you to get seasick if you stared at 'em long enough. The man was handsome as ever. The six-pack and the toned muscles in his arms and legs were only a plus. East was full of charisma and could hold a conversation for hours on several different topics. He hustled by choice, not being one to keep a job long enough to see any decent money. His cousin,

Papa, had been promising to put him on for years, but he could not wait on a handout from another man any longer.

East had been in the trenches, grinding, since he was released from prison. He'd done time over some petty shit. It all amounted to simply being at the wrong place at the wrong time, with the wrong motherfuckers at that. Spending four years in prison had taught him a valuable lesson about life, loyalty, and friendships. So now his outlook on life was that his life was his to live however he pleased, and he would kill a motherfucker before they tried to take him out. He was loyal only to those who expressed loyalty in return. He had no friends, because the few he kept around him were considered family.

Being locked up had taught him everything he needed to know. His whole routine had been switched up, and if he wasn't hustling, East was in the house or riding his bike with his cousin.

"Put your number in here," he said as he handed her his cell phone.

She tapped her digits in, stored her number under *N*, and gave him his phone back.

"*N*? Does it stand for *naughty* or *nice*?" East asked her.

"It stands for Nia. Don't know if you got . . . other things going on," she said, really wanting to know if he was single or not before she even thought of pursuing him.

"Nah, nothing going on but some money," East said confidently.

She nodded her head.

"Well, good night again, and thanks for the ride," she told him, and then she slid off the leather seat before she ended up sitting in his car all night.

East waited until she had started her car and was prepared to reverse out of her parking space before he pulled off.

Nia. I like her name, he thought as he made his way to Central Park. He had been renting a nice three-bedroom place, and it was costing him a pretty penny, but because he was obsessed with his shape, the park's scenic route was perfect for his morning runs. After he parked his car, he checked his surroundings, though he knew nothing was popping on the quiet street he lived on. East was sure he was the youngest resident, and his neighbors loved him, especially Ms. Deborah's married fine ass, who lived three houses down.

After turning the alarm off in his home, he tossed his keys on the table and went to his bedroom. The smell of the club was on him, and the first thing he did before even touching his Ralph Lauren sheets and comforter was shower. After he was clean and smelling good, he put on a pair of boxers and got into bed, turning on *SportsCenter* in the process. He thought about texting Nia to make sure she had made it home safe, but he had done enough tonight. Besides texting her in the morning to schedule their lunch date, he was going to fall back. The ball was now in her court. As cute as shorty was, he believed in mutual feelings and would not be the only one sweating.

He wanted Nia to crave him just as much as he wanted her.

After catching up on today's plays, he smoked a blunt and crashed out.

Nia stared at a sketch she had started for the third time since she made it to the office.

"This is not what this lady asked for," she said aloud to herself, snatching the page, tearing it out of her sketchpad, and tossing it, barely making the trash can.

She was struggling to sketch a dress for an actress who had been recently nominated for a Golden Globe Award. Nia was scheduled to meet with her Friday afternoon, and she didn't have anything on paper so far, nor did she have fabric or colors.

She hated when her mind drew a blank. She sat with the sketchpad on the design table and unlocked her iPad. She typed the chick's name into Google to get a feel of her style. It was important that Nia create the dress of the actress's dreams. She would want the same done for her special night.

Nia didn't really wear her own clothes. She was a denim and pumps girl. Today she wore an emerald jumpsuit with a jean jacket and a pair of Tory Burch sandals. She planned on sketching and catching up on her orders and gearing up for Saturday.

Her phone vibrated. She glanced at the screen and saw that an unknown number had sent her a text message. Because she knew it had to be East, she let the message wait until she finished her task.

An hour or so later, the same number was now calling. She was frustrated and feeling flustered, but she answered the phone, anyway.

"Hello?"

East chuckled. "Someone isn't having a good day," he commented.

"You're right. I'm not," she snapped.

He wasn't bothered at all by her attitude. East knew exactly what Li'l Mama needed.

"How about I bring you lunch, since you're tied up?" he suggested.

Nia was hungry, and she had been locked up on the third floor all day and had instructed her staff to hold all calls.

Her voice softened. "Well, I would like a spinach and chicken sandwich from Panera," she said kindly.

"You're something else. Okay. Anything else?" he said, making a mental note of the order.

"A bowl of the soup of the day, whatever it is. We have water here. Can you get me two lemons?"

East told her he would get everything and would see her soon, and she disconnected the call and got back to work.

About thirty minutes later, Kate's voice came over the intercom. "Nia, someone is here for you. . . . It's a man," she said, unable to hide her surprise.

Nia laughed, and over the intercom she heard East's hearty laugh as well.

"Oh God, Kate. Send him up, and can you bring us two waters?" she said.

"Yes, ma'am," Kate told her.

Nia searched through her purse for the roll-on stick of perfume she kept in her purse to spruce herself up. She dabbed her wrists and behind her ears as well.

Minutes later the elevator chimed, and Kate walked off first, with East in tow, carrying a brown paper bag labeled PANERA BREAD, her favorite place to have lunch.

"You look nice," East said after he stepped into Nia's office behind Kate.

Nia could not help but give praise where it was due. East was looking good as hell in the Nike basketball shorts and shirt and tennis shoes. "You look nice too," she told him.

"Not better than you," he said, winking at her and handing her the bag from Panera.

Kate eyed Nia, but she said nothing as she sat the bottles of water down on the glass table where Nia normally had her lunch while she was sketching. After Kate left, Nia pulled her chair closer to the table and began to empty the Panera bag of its contents.

"You're not eating?" she asked after noticing that the only thing in the bag was the food she had asked him to get.

"Nah. I got shit to do. Plus, we're going to dinner tonight," he told her, without even asking her if she was free.

She took a spoonful of the soup, even though it was too hot to eat right now.

"Oh, we are? How you know I don't have plans tonight?" she questioned.

"Postpone them. It's obvious you're a boss," he said, taking in the dimensions of the room.

"Something like that," she told him, downplaying her success.

Something she did often.

"What do you do?" he asked after he finally sat down across from her at the glass table.

Nia's mouth was full of two healthy bites of the sandwich. She was starving. She gave him the "hold on" finger and finished chewing her food before she told him, "I design clothes and wedding dresses."

"Dope," he told her.

"And what do you do?" she asked, returning the question.

He stroked his beard. "A few things. How is the sandwich?" he said, changing the subject.

She smirked, knowing he was hiding the truth, especially if he hung with Harlem.

"Awesome, and thank you. It's my favorite," she told him.

He nodded his head and watched her eat. After a few moments, he said, "I can tell." He smiled.

"Anyway, what are you doing for the rest of the day?" she asked.

"About to go kick it with my grandmother, and then I'll wait on you to get done with work," he said, putting his hands behind his head.

She eyed her Burberry watch. "About seven. Is that too late? You're going to wait that long to eat?"

"You're worth it, Mama," he said truthfully.

She did not want to blush, but as fine as he was, she could not help it. Everything that came out of his mouth caused her to smile and feel like she was in high school, crushing, all over again. Crushing on Biggs at that.

Nia wondered if he knew Biggs, but she didn't want to dampen the mood by discussing the past.

"Whatever you're thinking about, it's not that deep," he said, having seen the frustration lines form across her forehead.

She snapped back to reality. "You think you know me already, huh?" she smirked.

He quickly told her, "Not yet, but I will in due time."

Nia wouldn't argue with him, because she knew it was time for her to live. However, she wasn't letting her guard down just yet. He wasn't going to get her so soon.

"I'll call you when I'm almost done. You can come get me from here," she suggested.

"Oh, so you do like the way I drive?" he asked, wanting to be sure.

"Uh, no, I don't, but I do love your car," she told him.

"I'm in something else today, but I'll be sure to pick you up in it later."

"Sounds good to me. Thanks for lunch." Nia was grateful, because whenever she was zoned out, she would go the whole day without eating.

She walked him downstairs, using the glass spiral staircase instead of the elevator.

"Have a good day," he told her when they reached the lobby. He wanted to hug her but opted out.

Nia smiled and got on the elevator, pushed the button for the third floor, and waved at him before the elevator doors closed.

Once she was back at her desk, surprisingly, a dress idea finally came to mind, and she ended up sketching it without hesitation and was satisfied with the style. After she scanned it to the computer, she began to play around with different swatches of color. Once she chose a color, she pulled out her fabric books and cut fabric to tape to the printed design.

As she was putting the cut fabric aside, her phone rang.

"What are you doing tonight?" was the first thing Samone said when Nia answered her ringing phone.

"Girl, I'm going to dinner," she told her friend.

Samone asked nosily, "Dinner? With who?"

Nia blushed, feeling like a high school girl with a crush on the new boy in her chemistry class. "You don't know him."

Her friend started coughing and wheezing. Nia assumed she was smoking.

"Girl, are you okay?" she asked.

"I think I'm having a heart attack," Samone struggled to say.

Nia jumped up, in panic mode.

"Oh my God, Mone! What's wrong?" she asked, hoping that she had time to cross the bridge and get to her.

"I can't . . . believe you are going on a date," Samone said and then burst out laughing.

Nia rolled her eyes and plopped back down in her seat. "Girl, bye," she told her friend and hung up the phone.

A date.

Nia was really going on a date, and she was *actually* looking forward to it.

3

I'm 'bout to give you all the keys and security codes.
'Bout to show you where the cheese,
let you know I ain't playin'.

– Jay-Z

Nia smiled at East as they dined at one of New York's most popular pizza shops. She hadn't expected to eat at a five-star restaurant tonight, nor had she thought he was going to slide through the hood. They had ordered a half pepperoni and half sausage pizza and a basket of hot wings.

"I haven't pigged out like this in forever," she confessed, then licked her fingers before picking up yet another slice of pizza.

East was full and couldn't eat another slice, so he pushed back in his seat, stretched his legs, pulled her legs into the middle of his, and rubbed his stomach.

"Pizza was good as hell," he told her, staring into her pretty eyes and at her oval-shaped face.

Nia was thicker than a motherfucker, and he loved that shit. She wasn't his normal cup of tea, but baby girl filled the pitcher perfectly.

"You can eat how you want to eat around me, Ma. I love the way you look," he told her.

Her eyes wandered as she was unable to accept the compliment. Memories of the years of dealing with her

up-and-down weight flooded her mind. Nia would be a
size eight one month and a size twelve three months later.
She was told that she rocked whatever she wore, but still,
she suffered sometimes.

East waved his hand in front of her face. "I'm right here,
Mama," he told her and smiled, bringing her attention
right back to where he wanted it, and that was on him.

"*Well*, in that case . . . ," she said, lightening up the
mood. She took a huge bite out of the pizza slice in her
hand and moaned as the cheese and sauce dripped on
her chin.

He struggled not to leap over to her side of the booth
and lick up the pizza sauce, but in due time he would be
doing much more with his tongue.

"So, your day was cool?" he asked, genuinely concerned
with how her day had gone.

She nodded her head and wiped her mouth with a
paper napkin. "Actually, it was great," she said and
smiled.

Wanting to get her lips moving more, and enjoying the
way her eyes lit up when she talked about her career, East
asked her another question. "So, you love what you do?
Like, you love that shit?"

"Do you love what you do?" she asked, posing the same
question.

He winked. "It keeps everything afloat. Nothing more
or less," he replied, answering her question truthfully.

She understood that totally and remembered that
Biggs used to feel the same way. However, the difference was that she was here to warn East to get out
before it was too late.

"What's the backup plan?" Nia asked him, praying that
his goals exceeded that street shit.

She was not in the limelight for a reason, but she
couldn't control that people clung to her like white on

rice. It would not be ideal for her to be dating a hustler. But the thought of actually pursuing a relationship with the man across from her sent her face into another wide smile.

"You have been smiling all night, miss. Can I take the credit for that?" he teased.

She fanned him away in an attempt to get her shit together, and then she put her game face back on. She didn't need to be all up on him. Nia wanted to be dated, loved, and respected.

"Not yet, playboy," she told him jokingly.

There was something about East that relaxed her. She knew men like him were bad news, but the daredevil in her told her to go for it. She was a woman with tons of patience and was well aware that good things came to those who waited. As long they stayed on the same page, she was good.

"What's after this?" she asked after taking the last sip of her water, while East finished his beer.

He raised an eyebrow. "Damn. I didn't think that far. I thought your phone was going to be going off every five seconds, and you were going to use any excuse to run up out of here," he confessed.

She shook her head. "No faith in me. I actually have something in mind," she told him.

East didn't waste another second pulling a fifty-dollar bill out of a gold money clip, standing to his feet, and pulling Ms. Nia up on hers. Together, they left the restaurant and continued with their date.

"Where to?" he asked once they were back in his car.

She fumbled with her phone to make sure the place was open. "Are you familiar with Zucot?" she asked.

He told her that he was not.

"Let me drive. I'm not good with directions," she said.

"You were the other night," he commented.

She smacked her lips and asked, "You don't trust me with your baby, do you?"

"I like to drive. Tell me where we going," he told her, and Nia handed him her phone, not in the mood to be calling off every turn.

"What we doing here?" he asked thirty minutes later, after they'd made it to the gallery.

She smiled and took her seat belt off. "Come on. It will be fun. I promise," she said and hopped out of the car.

After she paid for two admission tickets to the art gallery, the lady at the counter told her they would be closing in less than an hour.

"This way," Nia told East after he made a right turn, having seen something in that direction that captured his attention.

He had never been to an art gallery before, and he had to admit that the shit was dope so far. The tall, mint-colored walls were full of pieces and each told a story.

Nia walked up to him and took his hand in hers and led him to one of her favorite artworks in the gallery. She came here often.

"Damn," he said once he laid his eyes on the canvas. East had no more words for what was before him. It was just that beautiful.

"It's everything, right?" Nia whispered.

She knew exactly how he felt. When she first saw this painting, she felt the same way.

"How much this cost? I need this in the crib," he said.

Nia laughed. "Trust me, I've offered every penny I have. The artist isn't selling it," she told him.

"Nah. There's a price on everything. You ain't naming the right one," he said.

Nia probably hadn't, but it was rumored that the artist had married rich and was now painting only because she considered it therapy.

"What do you see when you look at it?" she asked, wanting to get a feel for where his head was.

Too many times women dated men because of what the men had or what they wore. Those days were behind Nia, and she now had her own stuff and didn't need a man for anything. The queen stood on her own two legs and paid her own bills on a monthly basis. Webbie's hit song "Independent" featuring Boosie and Lil Phat had nothing on Ms. Nia.

It was important to Nia that East was more than his pretty eyes and luscious lips. His interests and world-view needed to connect to hers. She desired stimulating conversations about life and all the things it had to offer, other than things that had a designer's name attached to them. She would not rule him out because of his criminal dealings, but he had to bring more to the table.

East stepped back and stared at the picture. He took a deep breath and cocked his head to the side.

She watched him intently study the painting. Her heartbeat increased with every passing second that he remained silent.

It was as if East was in the initial auditions for *American Idol* and needed to impress Simon, the way she was grilling his every move. His posture, his stature, even the few movements he did make—all were being taken in by her.

"It's life after death," he mumbled and shook his head.

In that moment, it was as if time stood still.

She looked at the painting and back at him. How could this be? How could he feel the exact same way she did whenever she visited Zucot?

She felt herself getting hot.

"I'll be right back," she told him abruptly, before walking off and going to the bathroom.

East wondered what had happened to her. She looked flushed and bothered.

"This shit is hot. I want this bitch in my bedroom," he said aloud to himself, wondering what the price tag would be on a picture like this.

Nia came back and asked him if he was ready.

"Can you check on the price for me?" he asked her.

"I'll try later," she responded.

Once they made it back to the car, he didn't want to end their night so soon. The clock had barely struck nine. However, Nia had yawned twice already, so he knew it was best that he headed back to her office so she could hop in her ride.

"I'm sorry. I feel like a grandma," she said, apologizing for the constant yawning and for rubbing her eyes, as he drove.

East's phone lit up just then, and it was time for him to handle his business, anyway, so the date was ending at the right time.

"I had so much fun," she told him truthfully once they were in front of the design studio.

East began to roll a blunt while she gathered her purse, jacket, and keys.

"Word? Me too, baby," he told her.

She blushed. *Baby?* It sounded good to hear that again, though the word was spoken by a different person, not Biggs.

"I'll see you soon," she said, lingering in his car.

East stopped fumbling with the wrapper on the Backwoods cigar and gave her his full attention before they went their separate ways. "Whenever you ready," he said and stared into her eyes, wishing he were taking her to his house instead of leaving her at her car.

"Just text me," she told him, not wanting to sound so thirsty. Nia yawned again and shook her head. "Let me get home," she said while opening the car door.

"Okay. Be safe. Text me when you get in," East told her.

She smiled and got out of the car. He waited until she had pulled her car out of the private parking lot that belonged to her design studio before he honked his horn, did an illegal U-turn, then headed to the hood.

Harlem had hit him twice with the emergency code, but East had been with his new boo, and whatever it was, he'd known his homie could handle it until they linked.

"Where ya at, blood? I have been calling you," Harlem said once East returned his call.

East blew smoke out of his nose and dipped the blunt into the portable ashtray that sat in his cup holder. "Trying to be en route to you. What's the location?"

Harlem laughed, knowing East had probably been knee-deep in some pussy when he'd called him earlier. "Where else?" Harlem said sarcastically.

"On the way," East told him and then hung the phone up.

He switched his music back to the Jadakiss he was vibing to from the Beyoncé that Nia had insisted on listening to when she first got into his ride.

Nia.

Her name alone was magical, and East was prepared to make her his. She wasn't with the games, and luckily, he was the realest nigga she would ever meet, so she was in good hands with him. He was not as tailored as she probably preferred her men to be, or so he thought.

East was completely unaware that Nia was the former girlfriend of Biggs, the most ruthless and the coldest nigga to hail from the grueling streets of New York City.

"So, when will we get to meet him?" Nasi asked Nia as they waited for their main entrées to come to the table.

Nia acted as if she hadn't heard her best friend ask her for the third time in the past week or so about meeting East. She wasn't ready to bring him around or speak about him just yet. They were still getting to know each other. Although she had seen East only once more since their first official date, he called and texted her on the daily, and she appreciated the gesture. Their schedules were both crazy. He kept late nights and slept through the day, while Nia was at her design studio at dawn and in bed by eleven.

He had promised that she would see him this weekend, and Ms. Nia Hudson was actually looking forward to seeing her friend . . . or boo, as he called her.

"One day," she finally mumbled after feeling Nasi's eyes peer into her soul.

Nasi shook her head and sipped on the glass of red wine that she had paired with the calamari and shrimp Alfredo she ordered for dinner. "He must be someone we know, right?" Nasi questioned.

Nia laughed and bit into the roll that she had been holding. After she swallowed, she said, "No, ma'am, you don't know him at all." She was sure of that.

Before Nasi had met her boyfriend, she was successful, and she loved to remind people of this every chance she got. Nasi had her own business and had been doing quite well prior to meeting Harry. Nia had had a successful business, too, before she met East. But unlike Harry, East was in the streets. Although his lifestyle and career weren't ideal, Nia wouldn't knock how he got his own money just yet.

They hadn't really talked about what he did, but she definitely had questions about the impact his career would have on her image and her safety, and on his too. As time had slowly but surely progressed, she had begun to care about him. Every time he called, if she was able to stop what she was doing, she would. Their conversations weren't long and drawn out, but the few minutes they did speak were just right for her.

East was concerned about her, and he always asked her how her day was and what was on her agenda. After dealing with so many different personalities in the fashion industry, Nia could easily detect if someone was acting in a way that was authentic or fake, and she knew East genuinely cared about her day-to-day activities.

The waiter arriving with their main entrees interrupted Nia's reverie. Once he had retreated from their table, Nasi eagerly picked up the conversation where they had left off.

"So, what's with the suspense? Okay. Answer me this, friend. Is he a boy toy or a husband in the making?" Nasi asked, propping her elbow on the table.

Boy toy?

Husband?

Nia had not thought that far ahead, but she did think that he was handsome and that he was a cool person. For right now, she was taking her time and getting to know him, and then she would go from there. It had been so long since she'd dated, and she did not want to jump into anything too quickly.

"He's a friend, okay? Next subject. Do you want to go to a movie premiere tomorrow?" Nia asked her friend.

Nasi rolled her eyes, but she did let this topic of conversation go. She and Nia had been friends for years, and she had always known Nia to be a very quiet and private woman. She was happy that her friend had finally become interested in someone. She and her boyfriend had tried to hook Nia up on several different occasions with some of his teammates, but Nia had declined every single time.

"Harry has a game tomorrow. Come with me. Movie premieres are boring," she replied.

Nia nodded her head, contemplating going to the game. "I'll let you know. My boo and I are supposed to be linking up, anyway." She stuck her tongue out in a teasing matter.

Nasi tossed a calamari in her direction. "I can't wait to meet him. Bring him to the game, and I'll get an extra ticket," she said happily.

"Honey, we will see," Nia told her.

Once they had finished eating and had their leftovers boxed up, both women decided that going shopping could wait until another day. Nia wasn't in the mood to shop, and Nasi was full and sleepy. Nia kissed her friend good-bye at the entrance to the restaurant, hopped in her Audi, and peeled out of the parking lot.

She phoned East as she sat in traffic.

He answered the phone on the second ring. "Hey, you," he said in a low tone.

"Did I call at a bad time?" she asked.

East blew smoke out of his nose. "Nah. Where you at?" he questioned.

"Just left from eating and am now in traffic. Where are you?" she said, asking him the same question.

He looked in his rearview mirror and saw Harlem pull up behind him, finally. East had been waiting on his man for about an hour and a half now.

"Around the way. What you doing tonight?" he said hurriedly, trying to wrap up the conversation, because it was now time to handle business.

Nia told him that she didn't have any plans.

"Cool. Let me wrap up what I got going on right now, and then I'm going to call you," he told her.

She said, "Okay. Cool."

East unlocked his car door so that Harlem could get in and told Nia, "Text me when you make it home."

"I will," she said, growing used to doing that for him, since he always asked her to.

She had heard the urgency in his voice and figured he had something going on, so she then said good-bye and disconnected the call.

Nia turned the radio up and made her way to her condo. She texted Nasi once she was home and told her that she would be going to the game with her tomorrow and would text her in the morning.

She put her leftovers in the refrigerator and went to change into something more comfortable. An hour or so passed and she didn't realize she'd drifted off until her phone rang loudly. She jumped up and grabbed the phone. The screen read East and there were a few cute emojis. She slid the bar across the screen using her thumb and answered the phone.

"Damn, Ma. You went to sleep on me?" East asked after hearing her groggy voice.

She yawned into the phone. "Just a nap."

"I'm on the way to you. Send me your address," he told her.

She checked the time on her cell phone and saw that it was only 10:00 p.m.

"I guess you can come over. It's not midnight yet," she told him truthfully.

He laughed into the phone. "I like that."

"I bet you do. Sending you my address now. Call me when you're downstairs and I'll tell the doorman to buzz you up," she said.

"Bet," he told her, and they ended the call.

Nia was a very clean person, so luckily, she didn't have to run around her condo, trying to straighten it up, but she did light a candle and open the curtains to show the skyline. The view from her condo was breathtaking.

She poured a glass of wine and sipped it slowly while she stared out the window. Nia closed her eyes and cracked her neck while thinking of Biggs. She missed him, but not as much as she used to. The days of her crying herself to sleep and speaking with a therapist were now behind her. There was something about East that made her heart skip a beat, just as her heart had whenever she was in Biggs's presence. She wasn't sure if East was as powerful as Biggs had been, but he sure acted like it.

Nia wasn't shying away from his advances or his straightforwardness when he told her that he wanted to make her his woman, but she had told him to take it slow with her, remembering that Biggs used to tell her all the time, "Nothing that lasts long comes easy, baby girl."

East texted her and told her that he was pulling up, so she called down to the front desk and gave them his name. In the corner of her living room was a large gold mirror that leaned against the wall. She went to check her appearance in that mirror. Although she wore a pair of black leggings and a camisole with no bra, Nia still didn't want to look crazy.

She refilled her wineglass and told herself, *Relax, Nia. Damn!*

It had been quite a while since she had taken a man seriously or even welcomed one to her home. It was too late to start regretting her decision now. East would be knocking on her door at any minute.

Knock-knock.

"Coming," she called, her voice going up an octave.

She took a deep breath and opened the door. East looked even sexier since the last time she saw him, and she could not help but smile and blush. He bit down on his bottom lip as he took in her appearance. She looked calm and relaxed. Her skin was glowing, and she looked happy to see him, so East was thankful that they were feeling the same way right now, because he was just as happy to see her.

He walked in, closed the door, and locked it behind him before pulling her in for a warm hug.

"You smell good," he told her, inhaling her neck before staring into her eyes.

Nia eased out of the hug as she said, "Thank you." Then she stepped away. She had to pull it together, because his every move and action was turning her on, and the nigga hadn't even been here for two minutes.

"Nice crib," he told her once he had made himself comfortable on the couch.

She turned on the lamp that sat on a glass end table before she sat down next to him on the couch. She picked up the TV remote.

"Thanks. So you want to watch Netflix? I think there's a game on, or we can play—"

East took the remote control from her hand and laid it beside him. He pulled Nia onto his lap and made her face him. She shifted in his lap nervously.

"What are you doing?" she asked him.

He smiled. She was too cute.

"How was your day?" he asked.

Nia took a deep breath. "It was okay. I didn't do much work today. I went to dinner with my homegirl," she answered.

East nodded his head and stretched his legs, and Nia moved up on his lap.

"I know I'm heavy," she complained, wanting to get up, but East placed his hands on both sides of her hips.

"You just right," he told her, staring into her eyes and smiling at her.

"Stop," she said, shaking her head.

He laughed and, acting clueless, said playfully, "Damn, Ma. What I'm doing?"

She got off his lap. "Wine?" she asked, resuming the role of hostess.

"Nah. But water will do," he said.

East pulled his gun out of his jeans and slid it under the couch once she had turned her back and walked into the kitchen.

"You got some food?" he asked from his spot on the couch when he realized that he couldn't ignore his growling stomach anymore.

"You want my food from earlier?" she called from the kitchen.

"As long as it's not pork, then hell yeah," he said, fiddling around with the remote.

Nia heated up her leftovers on a plate and brought it to him with a napkin and a bottle of water.

"Thanks, boo," he told her, and then he focused his attention on the television. Eventually, he dug in.

Nia took a seat at the end of the couch, rested her back, and watched him eat his food. She could tell by his relaxed demeanor and low eyes that he was high, and he had probably had a long day.

"Damn. Where that came from?" he asked once he had returned from taking his plate into the kitchen and washing his hands.

Nia told him that the leftovers were from a new Italian restaurant around the way. "Their food is great," she commented.

"We need to go there," he told her, and then he sat back down on the couch and pulled her closer to him.

East hadn't stopped his work early tonight for them to be sitting so far apart on the couch. He rubbed her back and squeezed her shoulder as she nestled against his chest.

"What's on your mind?" he said. He wanted to know.

She sighed and said, "What's *not* on my mind right now? Deadlines, new business ideas. I really want to launch a lingerie line. My boutique has to open on Saturday, and I have nothing to go in it. I have to fly out to Africa for a stupid fashion show." She rambled on and on about her sometimes stressful life.

East listened to every word and rubbed her back while she talked.

"So, what we gon' do about it?" he asked when she fell silent.

She turned around and looked up at him. "What you mean?" she asked, not understanding his question.

"All of that gotta get done regardless, right?"

Nia nodded her head, still waiting on him to explain himself.

"So, there's no need to complain, boo," he said. "You still gon' handle it, 'cause you a boss. So no need to stress."

East wanted Nia to learn how to chill more. He didn't stress about things that he had no power to change. Business was always business, and when it came to money, you sometimes had to suck that shit up and get it done.

"You're right. I just wish there was one more of me," she confessed.

Nia never complained to anyone about her busy schedule, because she never wanted to seem ungrateful for her blessings. She knew where she came from, and God had truly brought her a mighty long way, but whoever had said being rich and busy was fun was lying. Reality television had people confused. Nia worked day in and day out and very rarely took vacations.

"Nobody can do it how you do it. That's why you handle so much on your own. But I'm sure there's some folks out here that wanna help you," he told her.

She agreed with him, because East was definitely telling the truth.

"You're right." She exhaled and turned back around and snuggled up closer to him.

The duo decided to order a movie, one with Leonardo DiCaprio in it, and it actually turned out to be a decent movie. East had always been a fan of anything DiCaprio was in, so he was tuned in.

Nia fell asleep in the middle of the film. East draped a mink throw that was lying across the couch over her body and stretched her legs out, and then he rested his hands on her ass and watched the movie until it ended. He shook her gently while the credits rolled.

"Ma, come lock the door behind me," he told her.

It was nearing two in the morning, and East was going to go home and crash, just as Nia had done.

She mumbled something, but he didn't hear what she said.

"What you say?" he asked.

Nia sat up and wiped away the slobber that had pooled in the corner of her mouth. "Don't leave," she told him, having noticed that it had started to rain. And she didn't want to sleep alone, not tonight.

East knew nothing was going down tonight. He was just as tired as she was.

"Okay. Come on. I ain't sleeping on no couch," he told her, and then he waited on her to get up so he could stand and stretch his long legs.

She turned the television off, flicked the lamp off, and walked toward what he assumed was her bedroom. East grabbed his gun and checked his phone for any important missed calls. Thirsty thots weren't included in that category, so he put his phone back in his pocket and followed baby girl into the bedroom.

"Close the door," she mumbled as she turned the light off and got into bed.

He wanted to get a peek of her bedroom, but Nia had it dark as hell already. He had to pull his iPhone back out and use the light on it to guide himself over to what he would soon be calling his side of the bed.

East took his sneakers off, unbuckled his jeans, and took them off. He removed the watch he wore, along with the T-shirt he had had on since early in the day, and then he got into bed. He yawned and knew he would be sleep in a matter of seconds. Nia's bed was comfortable as shit.

"Good night," she said in a low voice, and he smiled and told her good night back.

Yeah, a nigga can get used to this, he thought to himself before rolling over on his side and closing his eyes and drifting off into a peaceful sleep.

The next morning East wasn't expecting to wake up at the same time as the sun came up, but Nia was an early bird. He tried to tune out her movements around the room as she got dressed for work, so he could keep sleeping, but it was impossible.

He removed the duvet from over his head and got a nice view of her ass in a tight pair of panties as she stood over her nightstand, texting or e-mailing on her phone. He wasn't sure which one she was doing.

"Morning," he whispered, but she heard him loud and clear.

She dropped her phone and exclaimed, "Shit! You scared me!" She held on to her heart.

East said, "You always jumping. Let me find out my sweet baby got a dark past."

She told him, "Ain't nothing dark about me," and she meant every word.

Nia did right by people, even when people didn't deserve her gracious ways.

"I hear ya, Ma," East said and sat up in the bed. He rolled over to check his phone for the time. When he saw the hour, he said, "It's so early." He yawned.

Nia laughed. "It's six thirty," she said nonchalantly, as if six thirty in the morning was no different than four in the afternoon.

East normally got home from handling his business around three or four in the morning; he wasn't an early bird at all. He lay back down now and closed his eyes. He was very sleepy and needed at least four more hours of sleep before he could head to his crib.

Nia took in his body and noticed that his arms and stomach were covered in tattoos. Biggs had been a tatted man, but not like East. East's body was also ripped, because he visited the gym frequently. She felt her pussy jumping, and she knew it was time for her to get dressed, and for him too.

"Come lie with me for a li'l minute. You ain't doing shit," he said. He pulled the comforter back and patted her side of the bed.

She said, "I have so much to do."

East understood all of that, but technically, they hadn't spent any time together last night. She had fallen asleep as soon as the movie got good, and in bed he hadn't even held her. Remaining a gentleman, he had stayed far away from her, and it had worked since her bed was big enough for both of them to have their own space.

"Come here now," he commanded.

She sighed, but she did obey, climbing into bed and laying her head on his chest. East draped her thigh over his and gripped her ass in his hand.

"Don't start nothing," she whispered.

He smirked, although she couldn't see him do it. She was warning him to stay in his lane, but her hands were roaming all over his washboard abs.

East squeezed her soft yet firm ass and told her, "Nah, baby, we ain't gon' do nothing we ain't ready for right now."

Nia appreciated his patience, but as good as he smelled and as handsome as he was, she knew that sooner or later she would allow East to have his way with her delicate soul and her precious pussy.

4

"Cause I've got everything I've ever wanted. . . . I don't need nothing else from you but the simple things."

– Tamar Braxton

Things were going too perfectly, and Nia was desperately looking for something to complain about, but she was unable to find anything. Her business was running without a glitch, and her spare time was being spent with the perfect gentleman. Slowly, the days of Nia going to bed with her dildo and her silver bullet between her legs, calling and screaming Biggs's name, and wishing he were there making love to her were disappearing.

In fact, the last few times Nia masturbated, she had found herself screaming East's name, and it had surprised her. They hadn't reached that level of intimacy yet, but she couldn't act as if the thought hadn't crossed her mind.

Without a doubt, she knew that he would be the man of her fantasies. She was taken by so many things about him, from the way he licked his lips when he looked at her, to the way he walked coolly out of her place of business when he checked in on her. She was smitten by East. Every day he was putting a smile on her face and doing something special to remind her that chivalry wasn't dead.

Little did Nia know that everything he was doing was brand new to him. East didn't know a thing about romancing a woman, but in his pursuit of Ms. Nia Hudson's heart, he knew he had to step things up, and he was okay with that.

It didn't matter how busy he got or what he had on his plate. Nia was a priority. Even if it was a two-word text message, he made sure to communicate with her daily, no matter how busy both of their schedules were.

Their dates weren't typical, and Nia always had something new up her sleeve to show him, especially since East took an interest in art. She was opening up his eyes to other things besides the streets, and he appreciated that.

They were different—not too much, though, since they shared the same wicked and torn background. Nia had raised herself and had had little support in her transition from a little girl to an adult, while East, who was a troubled child, had given his grandmother the blues and every single gray hair on her head. They both knew the struggle.

One thing that they definitely had in common was their ambition. Imagine two hustlers who lived by the motto "Sleep is for the weak" trying to make time for each other twice a week. Fridays had been designated their day, but lately, they hadn't been successful in linking up on that day.

Nia was always flying in and out of town, and East swore he couldn't keep up with her. She would be in New York on Monday and in Atlanta, Georgia, by Tuesday night. East had considered himself a frequent flyer and a trapper of the year until he met Nia. Shawty stayed on the go.

Here she was on a Saturday night, sitting at the bar, waiting on East to arrive. If he wasn't in her life, she would have hopped into an Uber to meet Samone and Nasi so they could pregame before attending tonight's basketball game, but she had just flown back into town, and only one person was on her mind, and that was *him*.

"What are you thinking about?" East asked as he came up behind her.

Nia damn near jumped off the bar stool she was perched on.

"You scared me," she told him.

He kissed her neck before coming around and sitting beside her. "That means you ain't living right," he said, schooling her.

"Life is great right now, actually," she informed him, and then she raised her wineglass to give a toast to herself for having a very productive week.

He smiled and took a few seconds to take in her appearance. "Looking good, Ma," he commented.

Off the top of his head, East could name a few things that he adored about her, but her style was definitely in the top three. The way she re-created looks from the eighties and nineties and put her own spin on them was amazing. Tonight she had donned a tight-fitting pair of overalls and nude pumps. People might roll their eyes at her outfit, but Nia rocked it well.

"Thank you, and you do, too," she said, returning the compliment.

Nia asked if he was ready to be seated. Before she boarded her flight, she had made reservations at one of her favorite restaurants, in hopes that by the time she landed, he would have said yes to her text asking him to link up with her tonight.

It had been a while since they had seen each other, and she was looking forward to catching up over great food and picking his brain a little more.

She was taking her time getting to know him, and East was doing the same, but neither of them knew that the other was looking forward to discovering what the future had in store for them.

"What makes you happy?" East asked her once they had been seated at a table and had ordered dinner.

Nia was taken aback by the question and didn't know how to answer. She took a sip of her wine and uncrossed her legs under the table. She flashed him a smile. "What makes you happy, sir?" She asked him the same question, curious to know how he would answer.

East chuckled. "You first," he said.

Nia tilted her head and tapped her chin with one manicured finger. "Outside of my business, I don't know. Shoes and clothes, I guess."

It saddened her to hear herself admit that she was unaware of what genuinely made her happy. When did she become solely focused on work?

"Family, seeing my niggas win, black men with their children, beautiful women grinding like yourself. All that shit makes me happy," East confided.

How could she compete with his response?

"Not money?" she asked.

He shook his head. "I've been broke too many times to depend on money to put a smile on my face," he told her straight up.

Never could she forget those days. They were the reason why she had migrated the way she had. And now that she had made it, Nia was very careful with investing, with managing stocks, and even with giving away enormous amounts of money to charities. Her family was full of petty scammers and crooks. And as a result, Nia wasn't quick to write a check, and she personally signed every single check that came from her company. There was no power of attorney over any of her finances. She didn't play that shit.

The horror stories she had heard about assistants, managers, and accountants taking money and moving it into their own accounts had always been enough for her to set time aside to stay on top of her funds. Everything that went out and anything that came in had to be approved by Nia.

The waiter delivered their salads to the table, and after that the conversation shifted to their favorite basketball teams and who they thought was the best point guard in the league.

"Simple things make me happy, now that I think about it," she said a few minutes later, out of the blue.

East gave her a look of confusion.

"I couldn't stop thinking about your question," she told him, explaining herself.

"Simple things, such as?" He wanted to know for future reference.

She took a bite of salad, chewed, and swallowed before answering. "I love sketchpads. Although I have hundreds, I still buy a new one every time I am out. Bad habit, but drawing makes me happy." She shrugged her shoulders, not expecting him to understand.

"It's your therapy, huh?" he asked, loving how her face lit up at the mention of her favorite pastime.

She looked up and blushed.

Maybe, just maybe . . . he gets me, she thought.

"It allows me to get away from my thoughts. After a long day . . . man, all I need is a cup of coffee, a pencil, and my sketchpad," she said happily.

Designing was her life: drawing, sketching, sewing. It was her peace, her calm in the middle of a storm.

She went on. "Little things make my day. Chanel, Prada, all that shit . . . I can buy that myself. It doesn't impress me. Go to the art store and buy me some paintbrushes," she told him.

East nodded his head and made a mental note.

Simple things make her smile. Noted.

5

"Where do I go? When my heart's a broken record."

−Tamar Braxton

Nia ignored East's call for the umpteenth time. She didn't have time for games or bullshit, and it was best for her to cut things off before her feelings became even more serious and she couldn't find her way out.

She couldn't summon the energy to undress. She stood in six-inch heels at the living-room window, staring at the view, which was one of the perks of living up high in the sky in New York City. The plum- colored dress she wore was one she'd designed herself and was new. It hadn't even hit her boutique yet, and she had looked forward all week to modeling it for East.

Nia had even left the office early to prepare for what would have been date night. She had stopped by MAC and had asked for a natural glam face, and her stylist had curled her hair at his home, since he had not planned to take any clients today. She had then come home and had taken a long bubble bath and had shaved the areas that needed to be touched up, since it had been a week or so since her last visit to the Brazilian wax place.

All day she and East had sent cute text messages back and forth, and she had even sent a few selfies before and after her bath. She had had two glasses of wine, which had turned into three, as she waited for East to call and say that he was either en route or right outside, awaiting her arrival, but the call had never come. The call never came.

He hadn't even bothered to respond to any of the six messages that she sent him, asking about his whereabouts. Nia Hudson was a busy woman. In fact, she had canceled not one, but two different engagements for tonight, claiming that she had prior plans that were more important.

East was important.

Nia had moved her schedule around for *him*.

The nerve of that ignorant bastard to ignore her calls and messages. Did he not know that he was dealing with one of the most fragile minds on God's green earth?

Nia was a thinker. She evaluated and processed her every move. Like a chess player, she didn't do anything without much consideration.

Talking to East, allowing him into her home and her bed, was a decision she had made prior to it occurring.

Going on dates with him, answering his questions truthfully, adjusting her schedule, being transparent with him when they spoke over the phone . . . not everyone was given those opportunities.

She was closed off, reserved, reclusive, and quiet. She was also torn, bitter, and hurt.

Her heart had been ripped from her chest many years ago due to losing her lover unexpectedly, and ever since then, love hadn't been in her forecast. She had not put it on her agenda for the year. And dating, falling in love, blushing, smiling, pussy getting wet, or answering the phone on the first ring—those were not a part of the ten-year plan she had established.

East had special privileges, but they had been revoked.

She believed that if she allowed him to get away with disrespecting her this one time, then a pattern would be formed, and she was too old and too damn busy to be playing games with a grown man.

He had said he wanted her, but now she thought otherwise. She rolled her eyes as he called her again. The time read 3:21 a.m. on her cell phone and on the gold clock that was on the wall in the living room.

Half of her was curious to know what had possibly kept him from her, and the other half wanted to block his number and go to sleep.

However, she wanted him. She missed him and had been looking forward to tonight's date, and judging from his tone earlier, so had he.

So, why had he stood her up?

A knock at the door caused her to turn on her heels. There was no way he had made it through security. Nia paid a pretty penny for the fact that it was almost impossible to enter the building without a pass or granted access.

She knew it was him, because no one but East would dare show up to her crib without calling first.

East was one of those men who didn't give a fuck about following rules or having home training. He had checked Nia a few times and would probably do it again . . . if she opened the door.

Knock, knock.

He knocked again, but she didn't move from the window.

She unlocked her cell phone and clicked his ten digits, since she had deleted his number around ten p.m.

"Why are you at my home?" she asked as soon as he picked up.

"I know you're mad at me, but come here, baby," he said.

The fact that his tone was relaxed bothered her. Nia was thirty-eight hot, and he sounded cooler than a cucumber.

"No, so leave," she commanded.

"I'm not going anywhere until I see your face. I want a hug and kiss," he responded.

She let out a snicker. "Nigga, please. It was good knowing you, though," she told him.

East began to bang on the door.

Before his banging brought unwanted attention to the floor she lived on, she trekked across the hardwood floor and opened the door so fast that East stepped back. The scowl on her face caused him to pause. All the things he had planned to say now did not make any sense, and he was speechless.

"I don't play these games, and I told you that," Nia said, with one hand on the doorknob and the other holding her glass of wine.

"And I'm not playing any. Some shit came up totally out the blue," he said, explaining himself.

She was unfazed.

"A text message would have been nice. We've postponed before," she told him.

East wanted to come in and talk. "Can we talk about this inside, please?" he asked, not feeling like discussing his business in the hallway. He didn't know who the fuck stayed in her business.

"I'm not playing with you," she said. She was dead-ass serious about letting this thing go, even though everything had been great so far.

"I'm not playing with you, either, and I haven't played with you, but I can't control certain situations, and tonight I had no control over what happened." He held his hands up, as if he was surrendering to her.

"I liked you," she blurted out.

She was tipsy, and East could tell. Her eyes were low, and her shoulders were slumped over a little. Her hair was now pulled back from her face with a scrunchie.

"You still do." He winked at her.

Nia rolled her eyes and moved away from the door, then walked into the kitchen to refill her glass. East moseyed his way into her condo and locked the door behind him.

He took a seat on her couch and removed his sneakers. If only Nia knew how crazy tonight had been, she wouldn't be giving him such a hard time. When she joined him on the couch, he pulled her legs onto his lap and removed her heels.

"Nice," he commented as he sat the designer pumps on the floor.

"Brand new, just for you," she snapped.

He ignored her and began to rub her feet. "You know I'm going to make it up to you. One pass, Ma. That's all I'm asking for," he pleaded.

Because he had big hands and was massaging the hell out of her feet, she kept quiet and rested her head against the pillow, allowing him to apologize in any way that he could.

"I missed you, and you look beautiful," he said minutes later, breaking the silence.

She gave him a dry "uh-huh" in response.

Nia had forgiven him after seeing the sincerity in his eyes, but she would not show her hand too fast, as she was enjoying how much he was kissing her ass.

"Did you eat?" he asked. East was high as hell and was dealing with a serious case of the munchies.

Nia told him no.

"Well, what we gon' eat? What's open around here?" he asked, knowing that if they were in the hood, they would have a few options.

"Nothing but legs, but you messed that up, buddy." She laughed.

"I'll take anything right now, baby. I'm starving," he said and took one of his hands and rubbed his flat stomach.

Nia removed her legs from his lap and hopped off the couch. "What about fried egg sandwiches?" she suggested.

East was down with that. It had been a while since he'd had one, anyway.

"Make me about three of 'em," he told her.

She went to change into something more comfortable, and before she could return to the kitchen to cook, East came into her closet and peeled the dress off for her.

"I apologize," he said quietly.

"Just don't let it happen again," she said after two minutes of not saying anything.

Nia turned around and faced him, standing there in nothing more than a slip, her breasts bare and nipples at attention.

"I don't do well with bullshit. My tolerance is zero," she informed him.

They hadn't discussed her past or his, and quite frankly, they both were uninterested in the past. Focusing on the present was what worked for them.

East hadn't asked the questions most niggas asked when they were trying to get a feel for who they were fucking. He trusted that Nia had told him what he *needed* to know, and that was enough for him.

He ran his finger across her nipple and smirked at the reaction he received from the slight touch.

"Same here, boo," he said, letting her know that he, too, wasn't into games.

As bad as she wanted him to bend her over and fuck her till her knees became weak, her feelings were crushed, and his transgression couldn't be forgotten so easily, no matter how good he looked, how great he smelled, or how much he was awakening her hormones as his hands passed over her exposed frame.

Time was of the essence, and Nia had always been a woman with patience.

She trusted that everything would happen at the perfect moment, and when it did, she would succumb to his touch, his will, and his way.

For now, she stepped back, winked in his direction, and left him alone in her closet with a hard dick and a bruised ego, not used to being turned down.

East would soon realize that capturing Nia Hudson wouldn't come easily, but she was worth the wait and the chase.

6

"You know what it's gon' take, so stop playing with your
boy. . . . You know I don't got shit to prove."

– Chris Brown

On a rainy Tuesday afternoon, Nia was nestled in the
comfort of East's home. She had opted out of going into
the design studio today and had gone to chill with her
beau instead. He hadn't said two words to her since he
let her into the house earlier that morning. He had shown
her the living room and then had gone back to sleep.

She was surprised to see that his kitchen was completely stocked with groceries, considering he was always
out of town or in the streets. She whipped up a batch
of pancakes and about six strips of turkey bacon, since
East didn't have any pork in his house. Nia ate her food
quietly, alone, and finished it with a glass of orange juice
before cleaning the kitchen and putting a plate in the
microwave for East. Then she powered on her laptop and
got comfortable on his black leather sectional and got to
work.

One of the perks of owning her own business was that
there wasn't a clock she had to punch. Today was one
of those days when Nia would rather wear her Flyknit
sneakers and joggers instead of the custom-tailored pants
and the silk blouse she would have probably thrown on
this morning. Her hair was French braided, and her face

bore no makeup. She had doused herself with perfume. East was a sucker for her Bond No. 9 perfume, so she had begun to wear it often.

She was knee-deep in a sales report when his nose tickled the side of her face. Nia took her glasses off the tip of her nose and turned around to face him.

"Someone is finally up," she said cheerfully.

She had missed him. It had been a while since they had seen each other.

East stretched, causing his dick to jump against the Polo boxers he wore. It was actually the only thing he had on besides white Nike ankle socks.

"I was tired. Hell, I still am, but it was smelling so good in here," he told her, and then he walked into his kitchen.

"Damn, babe! You ain't make me nothing," East shouted from the kitchen. He sounded so disappointed. When he was out hustling, he barely had time to eat anything, let alone a home-cooked meal.

Nia shook her head, even though he couldn't see her. She put her laptop down and went into the kitchen.

"Nia, I'm hungry." East's grown ass was pouting.

She ignored him, pressed the thirty-second button on the microwave, and searched his counters for a paper napkin.

In anticipation, East took a seat at the kitchen table. "My nigga," he said happily as a plastic plate came toward him with a stack of pancakes and strips of bacon.

"Enjoy," she told him, eager to return to her laptop.

He wanted to let her work in peace. East had calls to return, anyway. And he had been out of town for six days, so he needed to go check on a few things and pick up some money. Never had he left a woman alone in his home before, but he knew Nia wouldn't go snooping around. Nor did he have to worry about her setting him up or trying to steal some shit. That was one of the things that he liked about her. She was very independent. And so was he. The good thing about them both being independent was that they didn't have to worry about who was with whom for what, meaning she had her own and he had his own.

Nia wasn't egotistical, and she allowed him to be the man in their courtship, or whatever it was that they had. However, he was starting to feel like Nia was friend zoning him. They had shared only a few kisses in the past two months, and when they did go to dinner, they talked and laughed like long-lost friends.

He knew that she was feeling him, and he was for sure feeling her as well, but what now? East wanted to progress, physically and spiritually. But she was harboring something, and he knew that she wouldn't talk to him about it until they crossed a few more bridges.

"Nia," he called after he put his breakfast dishes in the sink.

Nia waited until she had finished sending a very important e-mail before she went into the kitchen. "Yes?" she said as she walked in.

He couldn't help but smile at her soft voice. She was such an angel to him.

"Come here," East commanded.

"I thought you said you wouldn't bother me while I was working," she teased, walking into his personal space and touching his face, grazing his eyebrow with her fingertip.

He kissed her lips unexpectedly, and surprisingly, she didn't pull away, something she normally did when he caught her off guard and was feeling frisky.

"Where did that come from?" she asked minutes after the kiss ended.

He pulled her in closer and gripped her ass using both of his hands, because baby girl did have a handful. "When you gon' stop playing with me, Nia?" he asked her, wanting the truth.

She lowered her head, something she did often.

He waited on her answer, knowing that this would determine his next few steps with her.

"What am I doing wrong, East?"

He shook his head. "You not doing nothing wrong, but we both know that you holding back from me," he said. He kept it real and expected her to do the same.

Nia sighed and dropped her hand on his shoulder. She tilted her head and stared in his eyes. They were full of promises, but what happened when he changed? She was enjoying the cat-and-mouse game she had been playing with him, but she was worried about what came next.

A relationship with him sounded good. It sounded promising, but then what? The life he lived didn't technically align with hers, but neither had Biggs's life, and she had fallen in love with him.

There I go again, comparing the two men, Nia thought. They were different, and yet she found herself comparing the two often.

"Tell me," he said, pressing.

She stepped back, leaned her thick and voluptuous body against the granite counter, and crossed her arms. "Okay, don't get mad. Just listen to me," she began. Nia wasn't good at expressing her feelings. She was good at concealing her emotions and controlling how she felt.

East was not. He popped off when he felt disrespected, and he spoke up when he wasn't pleased with something or someone.

They both were grown and somewhat mature, so he felt it was time for them to lay all their cards on the table.

East sat down on a kitchen chair and watched her intently.

She cleared her throat. Her palms felt clammy. It didn't help that his eyes were drilling holes into her soul. "I'm scared, okay? I am." She tossed her hands in the air and walked away.

East called after her, "Come here. We not doing that walk-away shit."

His tone always caused her knees to go weak. She slowly turned back around, and East was not expecting to see a trembling and nervous Nia with misty eyes.

"What do you want me to say, East? I don't know how I feel. I don't know what you want me to do. I like you, okay? I like you a lot. Why do I like you? I am not sure yet. I cannot figure it out. You are always gone. You pop up at my office with roses and lunch. Then you call at all the right times. It's like you know when I need to hear your voice, and I . . . It confuses me." Before she could continue rambling on, he stood to his feet and faced her.

East wiped her eyes and asked her, "Do you think you can trust me?"

He wasn't the king of lasting relationships. In fact, he wasn't even a relationship-type nigga, but the moment he saw her at Summer Jam, he was taken by her, and when he saw her pretty ass two years later in the club, talking to his man, he knew it was fate.

Nia was supposed to be his, and he would do whatever he needed to do to get her and ultimately keep her.

Sending good morning text messages and having midday FaceTime calls were not his thing at all. East dodged and blocked calls daily, but with Nia the tables had been turned. He happily sent her texts and called her. And whenever he was out of town, ducked off and getting some money, he would send her roses through his cousin and or a simple love note. He knew that Nia was on a level of her own, so he had to come with it, and so far, East had been doing an amazing job.

Nia wasn't easily impressed, but East left her speechless on most occasions. And he didn't brag about what he had. Nor did she feel intimidated in his presence. The way they both made each other smile was a plus on both accounts.

"I want to trust you," she admitted.

East said, "Okay. So do it. If I fuck up, you can go about your business. I promise."

Nia's mind and spirit battled back and forth. She was nearing thirty and wanted kids. She desired commitment and marriage. She wanted a travel companion, a buddy to sit in the front row with at the games and to pop bottles of champagne on New Year's, then seal it with a kiss.

"Okay," she whispered.

East lifted her head, which she had lowered again, so they could look at each other as they made a promise to trust each other and not play any more games. "I couldn't hear you," he told her.

"Yes!" she screamed, and then she burst out laughing.

Finally, years after Biggs had left her, Nia felt like she had set herself free. No longer would her heart belong to Biggs. Although she had reserved a special piece of it for him, it was time for her to move on, and East was the perfect candidate.

"Whoever you're fucking, gon' and cut 'em off," she said, poking him in the chest.

As if she was the only one in his call log, he nonchalantly responded, "No worries, love."

Nia wouldn't trip on him. All she had was his word, and he had hers too. Until he proved her wrong, she would be optimistic. He had not given her a reason to question his actions or whereabouts, so she would be cool.

After their conversation ended, East went to shower and get dressed. After he slipped on clean clothes, he went into the living room, where Nia was working away again.

"How much more you got to do today?" East asked her.

Nia was on the phone with Kate, the secretary at the design studio. She motioned with her finger for East to give her a minute to wrap the call up. He sat down at the other end of the leather sectional and began to roll a few blunts for today. He needed to get a haircut, run errands, and slide through to see his grandmother. East had been slacking lately on spending quality time with his first lady, and he knew she was probably feeling some type of way, because she hadn't called him in two days. His grandmother was funny like that.

"Okay, I'm sorry. Kate couldn't find a sketch that needed to be approved by a client," she told East after she ended the call. Even though she was off the phone, she was on her laptop again, typing away.

Busy body, he thought to himself as he watched her continue to handle business. It was a slight turn-on, dating a boss bitch.

"I wanted you to ride with me today," he told her as he broke a bud of weed down.

Nia nodded her head, but she had no plans to leave the comfort of his own home today. "I was going to make us lunch in about an hour," she told him, hoping he would change his mind about heading out.

East laughed. "Good try, but I got shit to do. Come on, Ma. Roll with me," he said, hoping she would get her fine ass up so they could go.

She looked at her laptop and back at him. He wasn't looking at her, though. East was focused on rolling the blunt so he could get blazed.

"Where exactly are we going, East?" she questioned.

"Everywhere, so bring your iPad and notebook or something," he suggested, and then he got up to take the phone call that he had been waiting on. "Ten minutes, Ma," he said over his shoulder and then went back into his bedroom.

Nia finished up a blog for her Web site on what was new that month in the fashion world. She had recently become obsessed with Essence Murjani, a new jeweler who had hit the scene. Nia had copped a few of her necklaces and planned to order one with East's name on it soon if things went well.

She sent the blog to her editor and then went through her e-mail for styling consultations. She rarely took on new clients, because her schedule did not allow her to. For the past few months, she had been going back and forth with the idea of launching a style consultation company and contracting other stylists. She would offer the stylists a sixty-forty split. They would have access to her network, and in return, they would pay her a commission. If only she had twenty-four *more* hours in the day, she would have launched the company already, but she knew that right now wasn't the time to start a new venture. Nia didn't rush into anything. She took her time and did ample research to make sure that any business she wanted to start would be worth her time and brand and, most importantly, would be profitable.

Any real hustler knew that in order to make money, you had to spend it, but Nia was not in the business of wasting any coins. She spent money wisely.

"Let's ride, Li'l Mama." East's voice took her away from her thoughts.

Her beau was dressed in acid-washed jeans by Rock Revival, a black T-shirt topped with a jean jacket, and construction boots.

"You're not hot in all those clothes?" she asked him.

He helped her off the couch and told her, "Nah, boo."

They hopped into his Range, since he wasn't in the mood to ride low today, peeled away from Central Park, and headed to the hood.

"What's the first stop?" Nia asked.

Instead of answering, East turned up the newest Curren$y mixtape. He had something important on his mind, and it was better if they rode in silence.

Nia took the hint. She put her seat belt on and got busy on her phone. Business had to be handled today, whether she was at the office or not.

About thirty-five minutes later, they made it to the first destination. East needed a haircut bad.

"Come on," he told her as he turned off the truck.

"You want me to sit in the barbershop with you?" she asked, not understanding why she couldn't have just stayed at home while he ran his errands.

East got out of the truck and came around to her side and opened the door. "You gon' be giving me a hard time today, aren't you?" he inquired.

She smiled and pecked his lips. "Maybe," she teased as she grabbed her Céline bag and iPad. Nia hopped out of the truck and followed him across the street and into the barbershop. "I haven't been to Queens in so long," she whispered.

"What you know about Queens, shorty?" East asked. He really wanted to know.

She raised an eyebrow but remained silent. She took a seat on one of the chairs in the waiting area, while East sat down in his barber's chair.

Though she got right to work on her iPad, it didn't take long for Nia to notice that people in the shop were admiring her outfit. The good thing about being considered a fashion icon in today's fashion industry was that no matter what she wore, she somewhat killed it. Even in gray joggers, lavender and teal Flyknit sneakers, and a white T-shirt, Nia was looking fly. One of her wrists had a silver Burberry watch, while the other had a simple silver diamond bracelet, a gift from a dude whom she called herself dating about two years ago.

Nia put her iPad aside and placed a call. She glanced over at East while she was talking. He winked at her as his barber draped a cape over his body and began to brush his hair so he could cut it and line him up. Nia smiled at him, crossed her legs, and went right back to work.

"That's you?" the barber asked minutes later.

East told him, "Yep," and left it at that. Nia wouldn't be a topic of conversation, ever.

"Shorty looks familiar, real familiar," the barber commented.

East ignored him and checked his text messages.

Nia felt herself getting angry but tried to preserve her professionalism as she spoke on the phone with Janelle's manager. Janelle was the new "It Girl" around the fashion scene, but she was a bitch! Every time Nia sent her something, Janelle had a complaint, and Nia was growing tired of it.

Nia wasn't being paid at all for her efforts to reach out to Janelle, and the only reason she dealt with the chick was that her designs got good exposure when the hottest model wore them, and this exposure ultimately translated into increased sales and more publicity for Nia's brand.

Janelle's manager yelled into the phone, "Nia, I asked you for denim on denim!"

Nia pinched her nose. "And that's what I sent."

Janelle's manager cackled into the phone, as if Nia had told one of the funniest jokes in the world. "You think Janelle is going to wear something that looks like it came from the Goodwill?"

That was when Nia Hudson, fashion maven, became li'l Nia from Brooklyn.

She jumped up from her seat and paced the floor. "You know what? Send me all my shit back. Janelle does not have to wear another fucking thing that I make. I'm good on it," she told the manager and hung up the phone.

East rose in his seat, motioning for his barber to hold up. He walked over to Nia.

"Yo, Ma, you good?" he asked her.

There weren't that many people in the barbershop, because it was raining, but the few who were in there were all ears and eyes.

"Yes," she told him quietly as she sat back down in her seat. She went back to texting furiously.

She couldn't believe the nerve of that ho. She sent every call to ignore before deciding that Janelle's manager needed to be put on the block list. Nia was as sweet as peach cobbler, but she was not a pushover and did not tolerate disrespect at all.

East walked back over to his barber's chair, dapped his barber up, and handed him a fifty-dollar bill.

He and Nia left the barbershop, climbed back in the truck, and peeled away from the block.

Little did they know that East's barber, Fifty, turned to the other barber in the shop, whose station was right across from his, and asked, "Didn't that girl look familiar?"

The other barber nodded his head. "Son, I was thinking the same thing."

Fifty scanned his brain but couldn't come up with nothing. He knew that smile, though. He knew it well.

"What happened?" East asked as he and Nia cruised down the street.

She told him the story, and he shook his head.

"Don't give that ho anything else," he told her, getting mad at how people were taking advantage of her kindness.

Nia was nice, and he knew how she was, but he was about to toughen her ass up.

"I'm not going to," she told him, surprised that he seemed so mad.

"Good. Now, put your seat belt on." He gripped her thigh with one hand as his other hand steered the vehicle.

The day went by pretty quickly, and by the end of it, she knew that when he told her he was busy, he really meant it. She was thankful that he respected her enough not to ride around with drugs or large amounts of money in the car when she accompanied him. As they drove, he told her that today was a light day 'cause he had his shorty with him.

"I bet it is," she told him after trying to stifle yet another yawn but not succeeding.

Nia was exhausted and needed a nap. He looked over at her droopy eyes and slouched shoulders. His li'l mama was sleepy.

"One more stop before I feed you," he said.

She nodded her head, leaned it against the window, and closed her eyes as East pulled into an empty parking lot and waited on his homie to pull up. Seconds later, Harlem reversed his ride in and parked next to East. East got out of the Range and hopped in Harlem's car.

"They weren't short. Who told you that it was going to be short?" was the first thing East asked when he got inside the car.

Harlem racked his brain for a name. "Korey is the one, and he said there wasn't any traffic over there for a week straight."

East said, "Well, I don't know about that, because the count was right, and he even asked me when I was dropping the rest off."

Harlem knew that something wasn't right, and that in due time, everything would reveal itself. It always did.

"Shit. Other than that, is everything looking good?" he asked.

"Yeah, so far. I got a few other things to check on, but I'll do that later. I'm about to get something to eat," East told his homie.

"Who is the chick?" Harlem had noticed that someone was in East's front seat, but he couldn't really see who it was, because East's windows were tinted dark.

East smirked. "Wouldn't you like to know?" He wasn't telling Harlem shit, but he knew that sooner than later it would come out.

"All right, playboy." Harlem chuckled.

East dapped him up and told him to stay safe before he got out, climbed back in the truck, and headed to get something to eat with a sleeping Nia beside him.

As he drove, Nia woke up, and they decided to grab takeout and go back to the crib to eat. She took two bites of the food and drank half a bottle of water before lying down on the couch and going back to sleep.

East had too much shit to take care of to be sleeping in the middle of the day. The man had a twenty-four-hour grind, so he put their food in the refrigerator, kissed Nia on the forehead, and headed back out.

Nia woke up to a pitch-dark house and complete silent. She figured that East was in his bedroom, playing the game or talking on the phone, but when she took a look, to her surprise, he wasn't there at all. She called his phone twice, but he didn't answer, so she shot him a text telling him that she was awake. Nia went to heat up a plate of food before settling in the front of the television and scanning his DVR for something good to watch.

Twenty minutes later, East texted her and asked her not to leave and told her that he would be home as soon as he could.

Home.

She wasn't surprised that he didn't say, "My house," but she was pleased that he wanted her there when he made it in. She was looking forward to making beautiful memories with him.

***

"Mmm," a moan came from her lips, and before she knew it, so did another one. . . .

East smothered her with his love, and she didn't dare tell him to stop.

"What are you doing?" she whispered when she came up for air. "What time is it?" she then asked. "I called you."

Nia was on a roll with the questions and comments, and he silenced her again with another long and passionate kiss.

"You missed me?" he asked her in a low and raspy voice when the kiss was over.

He came behind her and spooned her, then planted kisses across her collarbone and the side of her face. His hands could not get enough of her round brown bottom.

"Kinda," she replied, playing with his emotions.

"My dick got hard when I walked in and saw you in my bed and in my T-shirt," he told her in between stolen kisses.

Nia rolled over and cupped his face in her hands. "Oh, really?" She kissed him back, taking control of their make-out session. East let Li'l Mama do her. He was happy that she was finally advancing toward him. She had never, ever made the first move, until now. "You taste like liquor," she told him, then kissed his nose after they pulled away from each other.

"I had a few drinks," he said. His eyes were closed, but he felt her looking at him. "How did you sleep?" he asked.

She didn't answer his question. Instead, she went back to pecking his lips and rubbing his stomach. She was hot and bothered.

"What's on your mind, baby girl?" East asked after noticing that Nia's breathing had increased.

"Make love to me," she commanded softly.

He sat up and got a good look at her, since the light in the bathroom was shining into his bedroom. "You ain't ready," he smirked.

Nia removed his T-shirt, which she had thrown on so she could sleep comfortably. "I am," she told him with much confidence.

It had been quite some time since a real penis had been inside of her.

East kissed her lips as he squeezed one of her breasts and then fondled the other until her nipples grew hard and puffed out, staring right at him.

"Now," she begged.

"Lie down and spread those legs," he told her as he slid out of bed and went into the bathroom.

"Where are you going?" she whined, ready for the sexcapade to pop off. They needed to get things started while she was still in the mood and feeling courageous.

East ignored her question. "Play with it for me, Ma," he told her and closed the bathroom door.

As he undressed, he wondered if this is something he wanted to do. Pussy was nothing to him. He got it on the regular, and he received it so much that he turned bitches down on the daily.

However, as time had gone on, and the streets had become more and more ruthless, he had found himself in dire need of something more solid and serious. Nia matched his fly. She reached his standards, and on top of being beautiful, she brought something to the table when she sat down.

Even though they hadn't been talking forever, he knew a good woman when he saw one, and she was it.

But sex complicated things, and East hated to give shorty the business and then find that he was unable to be the man that she needed right now. So far, he had been on his p's and q's, but how long would that last?

Nia knocked on the door, taking him away from his thoughts.

"East, I'm about to go," she told him sadly, feeling extremely rejected.

He took a deep breath, wishing he was high. He opened the door, and there she stood, with his T-shirt back on.

"Why are you leaving?" he asked.

Her face held a scowl. "Really? I ask you to make love to me, and you run in the bathroom. I'm good, boo, trust me."

She threw the deuces up in his face and walked off. Not liking that at all, East jerked her arm toward him. She spun around, and they were now chest to chest.

"Yo, who the fuck you talking to?" he said.

Her eyes jumped, but she kept her game face on. "I don't have time for the games," she told him straight up, not liking that he had gone into the bathroom.

"Who's playing games with you, Nia?" He didn't even know what she was talking about; thus far, he had been nothing but one hundred with her.

"You walked away from me. Do you know how hard it was for me to tell you that?" she screamed.

"Tell me what?" East asked her, playing dumb.

"To make love to me!" she yelled at him.

East was pissing her off, and it was time for her to go home, before she went back to being li'l ghetto, crazy Nia.

He picked her up before she could say another fucking word and took her back to his bed, laid her down gently, and kissed her mouth while making his way in between her legs with his fingers.

She tried to close her legs quickly, but East warned her, "Nah, don't do that, Ma." Her heart was racing, but when he whispered in her ear, "You wanted this dick, so I'm about to give it to you," she closed her eyes and allowed him to have his way with her.

He was so graceful with her body, and he made sure that not an inch remained untouched before he finally entered her. With tears in her eyes, she slowly opened her soul and allowed him access to her. After her pussy was puffy and swollen from him sucking the life out of her, he placed passion marks from the crown of her head to the backs of her legs, from around her stomach to the inside of her thighs, then sucked every one of her toes.

East catered to every part of her body, and he made sure she felt his touch every time.

"Is it mine?" East asked as he stroked her middle softly.

She answered, "Yes."

Her pussy was calling his name as he broke her walls down with every push and stroke. East would have thought she was a virgin, but when she pushed him away so she could ride his dick, he knew that someone had taught her well, but he had more tricks up his sleeve for her.

"Is it mine?" he asked again once Nia was on all fours, back arched and ass up in the air.

"Yes, baby, it's yours," she shouted as he played with her pussy from the back.

Once she told him again that it was his, he slowly pushed his thumb into her ass. Nia looked back at him. She wasn't feeling that at all.

"You trust me?" he whispered, reaching down to kiss her forehead.

She nodded.

He pushed his thumb into her ass a little more, and he knew after the initial feeling, Nia would be loving it.

"Ooh," she groaned.

He replaced his fingers with his long dick and started to rock on the inside of her.

"Damn, baby. You not gon' throw that ass back on me?" he taunted.

Nia rested on her elbows and did as he asked, blowing East's mind. They climaxed for the third time before falling asleep.

In the middle of the night, Nia woke up to find East's arms wrapped around her body.

"I'm right here, baby," he whispered in her ear and pulled her even closer than she already was.

Although he was referring to him being near her, she prayed that East would be right there *with* her through it all. That was what she needed right now, a Clyde to her Bonnie, a rider, a best friend, a fan, a groupie, a cheerleader, a supporter and, most importantly, a true love.

7

"My life is a movie and everyone's watching. So let's get to the good part and past all the nonsense."

– *Justin Bieber*

"Hand me a pair of scissors," Nia mumbled. If her mouth wasn't holding two pins and a piece of fabric, then her assistant, Morgan, would have heard her.

Morgan bent down. "What did you say?" she asked her boss.

Nia pointed behind her, assuming that the young woman would automatically know she was asking for scissors.

"Which item? Measuring tape?" Morgan asked.

Nia rolled her eyes, got off her knees, and went to grab the scissors. She ignored her assistant and went back to working on the wedding dress, which had been hoisted up a few feet so she could hem the bottom perfectly.

"Box of pearls," she said fifteen minutes later, after realizing that the dress needed more pearls on the left sleeve.

Fourteen hours.

She had been on her feet for fourteen hours, putting the finishing touches on yet another wedding dress, number forty-one, to be exact. Nia had designed forty-one wedding dresses since her career started, and there wasn't one wedding dress that looked like another. She took her time, carefully designing each dress so that it was unique. Dress forty-one had to be her favorite so far.

Nia had put her all into this dress, and not because she was getting paid 100,000 dollars, which was her minimum. In fact, she was not being paid for this custom wedding dress at all. It was the best gift she felt she could give to her best friend, Nasi. Harry's ass had finally got down on one knee in front of close friends and family and had asked for her hand in marriage. Nasi had no idea that Nia had designed this dress, and Nia could only pray that her friend loved it.

"Okay, how does it look?" she asked her assistant.

Morgan stared at the dress, with admiration in her eyes. She was patiently waiting for the day that her long-time boyfriend asked her to marry him.

"It's beautiful, Nia," she told her.

The train was almost twelve feet long and made of nothing but lace and sheer fabric. The veil and garter band were handcrafted by Nia, and she had had his initials engraved on the garter as another special gift.

"When are you going to show it to her?" Morgan asked.

"Not sure yet. Nasi isn't rushing the wedding. Well, that's what she tells us."

Nia picked up her cell phone. She hadn't so much as answered either of her two phones over the past fourteen hours. When she was focused on a design, she wouldn't allow anything to distract her from her vision.

She saw that she had three missed calls from East, coupled with a few text messages from him, which were filled with emojis and questions about her whereabouts. Right when she was about to call him back, the elevator opened on the second floor of the design studio.

"I'ma get you." East's voice filled the room.

She turned around and let a wide smile spread across her face. "I was calling you back." She waved her phone.

He acted as if he was pissed, when deep down inside, he was happy to see his lady. She had been grinding all week, and he had too, so the couple hadn't spent any time together.

"It's Friday night, babe," he whispered into her ear after they shared a hug and a kiss.

"I know. I know," she told him, staring over at the wedding dress, making sure it was perfect.

"So, let's ride," he suggested, wanting to take her to dinner and to grab a few drinks before settling at either his house or her condo. East didn't care where they ended up. As long as he woke up to her beautiful ass, he was good.

"Where are we going?" she asked him, not even paying him much attention.

He pulled her close and wrapped his arms around her waist and kissed her neck. "I know you haven't eaten. What you got a taste for?" he said.

Nia melted in his arms, and as if her assistant wasn't even in the room, she turned around, kissed his lips, and said, "You," eyeing him lustfully.

"Shit. That's on the menu too," East told her coolly, resting his hands right above her behind.

"Morgan, close up, love. I'm out," Nia told her assistant.

She grabbed her purse, cell phone, shades, and keys and took East's hand in hers, and they headed out.

"I'm too tired to drive," she told him once they had made it to the parking lot.

"You gotta be here tomorrow?" he questioned.

"Boutique is open tomorrow, babe," Nia reminded him.

This week Nia had really worn an *S* for Superwoman on her chest: she had flown to Miami for a consultation, had appeared for jury duty, and had hired some young, fresh faces in preparation for her fall show, along with styling two clients, getting items ready for Saturday's opening at the boutique, and designing and sewing Nasi's wedding dress. Li'l Mama was officially tired.

"Yo, you need a vacation, and I'm going to kidnap your ass," East threatened.

Nia could not remember the last time she had gone out of town for pleasure and not work. "I so need that right now," she admitted.

"Wherever you wanna go, boo, we there," he told her, hoping that she would say, "Book the flight."

East thought he worked hard, but he did not work as hard as Nia, and the fact that she never complained and did everything with a smile made him want to give her the world. It was nothing for him to send a masseuse to her condo on a Sunday afternoon or to send roses to her job. He never wanted her to forget that her hard work wasn't in vain, and he wanted her to know that her efforts were noticed. He was proud of his woman.

"Come on. I'll drive. You can drive my car back up here tomorrow," he said and opened her car door, another thing that he had recently started doing.

Nia had East wrapped around her finger, and she didn't even know it, but it was definitely vice versa.

She had asked him on several occasions when the ball would drop. When would they argue or get mad at each other over something petty? However, it had yet to happen. Things were perfect, and every day brought a new feeling of bliss. East had told her it was because they weren't joined at the hip. Even when she was working and he was grinding, she always missed him, but right now, they both were focused on acquiring millions. It worked for both of them.

Nia got in the car, then placed both of her phones on silent and put her seat belt on.

"Babe, I want some steak," she told East once he was behind the wheel.

All week long she had been eating like a bird and drinking only coffee in order to stay up and finish the dress. Tonight she wanted a big, juicy steak topped with mushrooms and onions, a side of loaded mashed potatoes, and a drink or two.

"Okay," he told her, and then he headed to a popular steak house in downtown Manhattan.

"Damn. Who's here tonight?" she asked once they pulled up to the valet.

The front of the restaurant was loaded with paparazzi. She was not in the mood to deal with these annoying bastards.

"You don't have any shades?" she asked him after she placed her Céline sunnies on her face.

He snickered. "Bae, it's dark as hell outside. Why you got them shades on?" East thought she looked crazy.

Nia knew that he wasn't used to the cameras and shit being in his face, but she had been living in the limelight for a few years, and she had grown accustomed to keeping her game face on and making it to her destination without answering any questions or looking directly into any camera.

"Okay. You'll see," she told him and then allowed the valet attendant to open the door for her and let her out.

Because she knew her only task today was finishing Nasi's wedding dress, she didn't go into work dressed to the nines. Nia wore a gray T-shirt dress and black Chucks, and she had a plaid button-down tied around her waist.

East came around the car and took her hand in his. He was looking quite fly, but what else was new? Nia often joked that he had more clothes than she did, and he never denied her allegations. As time had gone on, shopping had become one of their favorite things to do together, besides lying in bed and kissing each other like lovestruck teenagers.

As they walked to the door of the restaurant, questions came at them from the left and right.

"Who's the guy, Nia?"

"Nia Hudson, who is the new man?"

"Boy toy?"

"Yeah, Nia. Is he your boy toy?"

East wasn't with that word, and he started to go the fuck off, but Nia pulled his hand and kept him walking toward the door.

"Who the fuck they calling a boy toy?" he asked her angrily once they had made it inside.

She took her shades off and told the hostess that they needed a table for a party of two.

"I told you it was going to be crazy. What? You thought I was playing?" she replied.

He walked off and went to the restroom, needing to calm down. He wasn't a fucking boy toy. He had his own shit, and Nia had hers.

This was the first time he'd ever seen people fawn over his girl, and he now understood that Nia wasn't *just* his down-to-earth chick, whom he kicked it with and brought lunch to when he was on that side of town. She was a celebrity. She had fans, and rude-ass, ignorant motherfuckers who called themselves paparazzi stalked her for real. Nia would call him sometimes and would yell loudly in the phone, complaining about not being able to enjoy a pedicure in peace or have a drink at the bar with her girls, because the paparazzi were swarming around her. East had always assumed she was being dramatic, but tonight he had seen the paparazzi's antics with his own eyes.

His girl was fucking famous.

After taking a deep breath and splashing some water on his face, he returned to the hostess station and asked where Nia was being seated. He was then escorted to a private room, and the door was closed behind him.

Nia had ordered a bottle of wine and a Hennessy for her man. She was tired and ready to lie down, but she was hungry more than anything.

"I'm sorry," she said, apologizing, once East took the seat across from her.

"What you sorry for?" he asked.

She sighed and took another sip of the Riesling wine before responding, "I know you live a private life, and mine is so public."

East hadn't thought that far, and he hoped that those people didn't go snooping around or try to match his tag number to a name or some shit.

"It's cool," he told her, dropping the subject, not wanting to talk about something that they both had no control over.

Like Nia, he had had a long day and was looking forward to enjoying their dinner, then unwinding back at the crib with a blunt and, hopefully, some head from his lady, if she was in the mood.

"I like this room, though," he commented, noticing that they were the only two people in the dimly lit room.

"Yeah, I just wanted to have dinner with you, not with a bunch of strangers," she said and winked her eye.

East smiled at her. "I feel you, Ma."

His phone was vibrating in his pocket, and he saw that it was his homie, Harlem, calling. "Yo," he answered.

Nia was used to his phone ringing off the hook when they were together. It didn't bother her at all. Her business wasn't as nonstop as East's. It was nothing for her to place her phones on silent and not check them again until the next day. Of course, she always made sure all her clients were squared away if they had an event before she went ghost on the world.

"Shit. I'm in the house tonight," he told Harlem after Harlem asked what the move was.

East chuckled and Nia figured whoever he was on the phone with had said something funny. She loved seeing him happy and smiling. Last week he had been complaining about there being too much sneaky shit going on, and he'd been saying that he needed to lay low. She had been worried that it would be a while before she saw him again, but apparently, everything had blown over. East had never brought the matter back up, and neither had she.

"What you looking at?" he asked her once he hung up the phone.

"You," she said.

"What's on your mind?" he inquired.

"That night I saw you in the club, you were with Harlem, right? You know him?" she questioned.

Rather than answer her questions, East sat up in the chair, because the waitress had brought out some fresh bread. She asked for their order. He nodded at Nia and told her to go first. He normally ordered whatever she did. His girl had the best taste when it came to everything from food to clothes to fragrances. East didn't mind letting her lead sometimes.

After she ordered the rib eye, East said, "Y'all got some shrimp?" He was so hood.

The waitress suggested mussels and shrimp over angel-hair pasta.

"Yeah, that's cool. Can I add a lobster tail?" he said.

The waitress added a lobster tail to East's order, and then she told them that she would try to have their orders out as soon as possible. Before leaving the room, she refilled their glasses with water.

"What made you ask me that?" East asked Nia, returning to their conversation.

She shrugged her shoulders. "Just a question," she told him.

"Harlem and I are cool."

East wasn't sure why he had lied instead of telling her the truth. He and Harlem were best friends and business partners.

Nia nodded her head and looked at him. "Why do I feel like you're not telling me something?" she asked.

Biggs had always told her to trust a man's eyes, and *hell*, a bitch's too. East's eyes gave him away.

East took a sip of the brown liquor. "That's my homie, my best friend," he said.

"*Okay*. And?" She wanted it all, because whatever he didn't tell her tonight, she would be calling Harlem tomorrow to find out.

"And what, Nia?" East was not feeling her tone at all.

She sat back and observed his demeanor. "What's up?"

Gone was the good girl; Brooklyn had appeared.

"You killing me right now." He blew out a deep breath.

"I'm saying, you are acting weird. Are you hiding something?" Nia could feel her attitude shifting, and she was getting very angry.

"Can we enjoy our dinner? I haven't seen you all week."

Nia rolled her eyes. "East." She said his name with an annoyed tone.

He liked to see her act up, because she rarely did. "Chill," he told her and held his brown hand out to take hers, but she didn't reach across the table and hold hands with him.

She was mad.

"How do you know Harlem?" he asked her.

She bit her bottom lip. "He doesn't know that we're talking, does he?"

"Shit. Last time I checked, we were both grown. Harlem your daddy?" he said sarcastically.

"He's family," she answered.

East raised an eyebrow. "Family like what? 'Cause I know his family, and I've never seen you around."

"Again, does Harlem know that you and I are talking?"

He shook his head. "When I saw you in the club that night, I asked him to introduce me to you, and he said no."

"And did tell he you why?" she asked, pressing for more information, anxious to find out what East knew about her past.

"He said you were his man's peoples, or some shit like that," he told her.

Nia finished her glass of wine in one gulp.

"We good?" he said.

East kept his cool, but he wasn't trying to lose the one good and constant thing in his life right now. He did not give a fuck who her peoples were, or who Harlem's were, for that matter.

Nia was his. Point-blank. Period.

"Did you know Biggs?" Nia asked, with a weird look on her face.

"Who the fuck didn't know him? He ran Brooklyn and every other spot. You gotta be living under a rock if you didn't," he joked, wanting to bring the joy back into the dining room.

This conversation was on track to ruin a perfect Friday night.

A soft smile came across her face at his comment. He was definitely telling the truth. Everyone knew Biggs. He was a motherfucking boss, and a real one at that. Nia was satisfied with his answer, because if he had said some sideways shit about Biggs, that would have instantly ended whatever they were slowly building.

Even though Biggs was no longer here, she would always respect his name and would demand that anyone in her presence did the same, including the nigga she was currently fucking.

"Yeah, I was his girlfriend. I was in love with Biggs until the day he died and for a few years after that," she confessed.

East dropped his glass of Hennessy on his jeans.

"Damn," he mumbled. He picked up the folded cloth napkin that lay at the edge of the table and patted his lap dry.

Biggs's girlfriend?

They sat in silence as East pondered this news, clearly perplexed. How in the fuck had East not put two and two together? He had seen her in the club, hugging Harlem's cousin, Biggs's brother.

"East, say something," Nia said, breaking the silence.

"Ain't nothing to say, Nia. That's cool," he told her.

Luckily, the salads that came with their entrées arrived just then.

"Another wine, please," Nia told the waitress.

East didn't say much of anything else for the remainder of dinner, and Nia had no idea what was going through his mind.

The car ride to her condo after dinner was quiet as well. When they got there, East made no move to get out of the car.

"You're not coming in?" she asked.

"I gotta go handle something," he said dryly.

She smacked her lips. "Okay. So you're coming back when you get done? I'll stay up," she said.

He shook his head. "Nah. Get you some rest. I know you tired."

Nia turned toward him, but he was looking straight ahead. "East, what's wrong?" she asked, wanting to know what had happened and why was he being so short with her.

"Nothing, shorty. I'ma call you."

She wouldn't kiss his ass. It was obvious that he wanted her to get out of his car.

"Good night," she told him sadly, and she made sure to slam the car door when she closed it.

East usually stayed on her ass about slamming his doors. Normally, he would wind the window down and playfully threaten to kick her ass, but he didn't do any of that this time. East made sure she was safely inside the lobby before he peeled into traffic.

He called his best friend and homie right away, but of course, Harlem wasn't answering the phone. Any other time the nigga picked up on the second ring. It wasn't too late for East to slide through his favorite person's house, so he headed there, hoping that Harlem returned his call soon.

After East dropped her off, Nia sat in her living room, finishing a bottle of wine by herself.

She could not deny the look on East's face when she told him that she was in love with Biggs until he died and then for years after. What was bothering her was that she couldn't decipher what part of her revelation made him uneasy or mad: the fact that she had been Biggs's girlfriend or the fact that Harlem had not told him this.

She was very confused. And Nia now knew for sure that she hadn't been tripping this whole time. She knew that things had been going too good, just as she'd thought. She took a deep breath and tried to put a more positive spin on things. She decided that as long as East didn't care about her past, she didn't, either. And technically, Biggs was in the past, and quite literally, he was no longer here on earth at that.

Embracing this newfound optimism, Nia stood up and headed to her bedroom. She was looking forward to wearing something sexy for her man tonight and giving him what she knew he had been missing. But unfortunately, Nia was going to bed alone.

She took a long hot shower, allowing the hot water to relax her muscles. After setting the alarm and turning off all the lights in her condo, she closed her bedroom door and got into bed.

East had a few pair of sneakers on his side of the bed and a few other things he had left. He'd joked that he was making his mark there for other niggas. Nia had told him on several different occasions that he was the only man in her life, and that as long as he kept it one hundred with her, things would stay that way.

Today while she had put the final touches on Nasi's wedding dress, the thought of marriage had crossed her mind. She and East seemed to be on the same page as far as being ambitious and becoming the best that they could be in their respective fields, but never had they discussed long-term goals and plans. After Biggs had passed, she had dismissed any ideas of marriage and children, but she now desired the finer things in life, and that didn't include foreign cars and a top-floor apartment overlooking the city.

Nia had acquired everything physical that was thought to bring happiness, but she now knew that this happiness was only temporary. She wanted to hear a replica of herself call her Mommy. She wanted to become a Mrs.

Because she loved living in the middle of everything happening in New York, the white picket fence wasn't in her dream life, but a nice home was. Nia didn't see herself retiring anytime soon, but she wouldn't mind slowing down to raise a few babies.

As her eyes became heavy and she felt herself falling asleep, she prayed that God would send her clear signs of her future, and she wondered about her and East.

Oh, how badly she wanted to be with him, loving and enjoying every minute she spent with him, but if they were not meant to be, Nia didn't want to waste any more of her or his time.

She rolled over and texted him, even though she had promised herself that she would not.

Hope you're safe, babe. Going to bed, with us on my mind. She added a kissy face emoji to the message before sending it off.

East read the message but didn't bother responding. It felt good knowing that his li'l mama wasn't mad at him.

"Was that her?" his grandmother asked. She was standing at the sink, washing today's dirty dishes.

He nodded his head as he stared at his phone screen, wishing he were holding her thick ass right now.

"So, what you gon' do?" she asked, hating to see her grandson look so down.

East had confided in her, had told her what happened with Nia, and she had told him how she felt about it. Although he trusted her with his entire life, he knew that his grandmother wasn't right about this particular situation.

8

"When I look outside my window, I can't get no peace of mind."

– Rihanna

Thumbing through the pages of her planner, Nia sat in a corner of her office, with a pen in between her teeth and the world on her shoulders. She was not having a good day.

Her business manager, Paulette, knocked twice on the door before she entered the room.

"We won the bid," she told Nia happily.

Nia wanted to jump up and down, scream and shout, cry tears of joy, and raise her hands to the heavens, thanking God. She had patiently waited on this moment for quite some time, but now that it was here, she honestly couldn't care less. The girl had been in a funk for weeks, ever since she and East broke up. East had simply distanced himself from her with no warning or real explanation, and that was enough for Nia to call it quits on the relationship. Nia didn't like how her peace and joy had been suddenly stripped from her, but she refused to call or text East any more than she already had and demand that they talk things over.

She dealt with the loss and the loneliness the best way she knew how, by working tirelessly. Nia had damn near moved into the design studio. Every morning she was up at the crack of dawn, and then she sewed for hours and hours, until her fingers bled and her back begged her to stop. Despite her grueling work schedule, she felt miserable and empty, and it showed. Her appetite had dwindled, and she had been losing weight by the day, and her spark for life had left her eyes. Stress and worry lines now creased her forehead.

See, the thing was, she had allowed him in. She had smiled and relaxed in his presence. And she had given him access not only to her body but to her mind and heart as well. He had been given the key to Nia Hudson, something no one besides Biggs had ever had, and so he had seen the real her, without the mask, without fronting. He had seen the Nia who was honest, submissive, quiet, and kept. The most innocent pieces of her soul, he had held in the both of his hands.

Feeling like a fool for falling so easily for him, Nia was disoriented, and she was struggling to find a happy place, a medium, a balance between who she was and who she wanted to be. Prior to meeting East and actually taking him seriously, Nia had never seen herself settling down with anyone. In fact, she had convinced herself that Biggs would be the only person she would ever love wholeheartedly. But East had come in like a strong wind. There was so much about him that she had clung to—from the way he brushed his teeth to how he laced his sneakers. She was astonished that he knew what she had a taste for, even when she didn't know herself. East was *it* for her, and she knew he felt the same way.

"Nia, did you hear me?" Paulette asked.

Nia nodded her head. "Yes. That's good. As soon as they send the budget, we will get started," she told her, with little happiness detectable in her voice.

Everyone around the office had noticed the change in her attitude and demeanor. Nia had never acted like this in the past five years she had been in business. Everyone knew that something had happened. But no one knew that the poor woman's heart had been broken. Twice.

Paulette sighed, but she bit her tongue, not wanting to upset her boss. "Yes, ma'am. I'll e-mail you the numbers," she told Nia. Then she walked out of her office and made sure to close the door.

As bad as Nia wanted to celebrate earning the title of head costume designer for *Belle*, the newest Broadway production, which was set to hit the theater next spring, she had no strength. Nothing in her cared about the accomplishment. Something that had always been a dream now was nothing more than another objective on her to-do list.

How had she allowed love to affect her passion, her paycheck and, most importantly, her career? she wondered.

It had been a while since she went to a fashion show or showed her face at any of the cultural events happening around the city. The only thing that she allowed to take her from work was helping with the planning of Nasi's wedding. Nia refused to be sour during the times she met with Nasi to get the wedding together, so she would wipe the tears away, powder her face, and handle business.

Once the weekend of the wedding arrived, Nia had no choice but to peel away her covers and head to Nasi's bridal brunch, which was strictly for her close female friends. It had been Samone's idea for everyone to get together to celebrate their friend being the first in the bunch to get the "prized possession."

"Are you okay?" Samone asked Nia when they met up at the bar during the brunch.

"I'm great." Nia gulped down the champagne and nodded her head. "How are you doing?" she asked her best friend sarcastically.

Samone eyed her curiously, wondering what was going on with her girl. She had not been right these past few weeks. She had been ignoring their calls, canceling lunch dates, and being extremely distant. Samone knew when Nia was going through something. They had been friends for quite a while now.

"Nasi looks happy," Nia commented, looking over at her friend, who was working the room, making sure to speak to everyone in attendance.

Tonight was her bridal shower, and of course, Nia, being the creative person she was, had designated herself the host.

"I've never seen anyone get married as fast as you," Samone teased once Nasi joined them at the bar.

Nasi rolled her eyes. "Bitch, please. As long as I waited on his ass to get on one knee, I'm not wasting no time," she said. She kept it real with the two people who she knew would never judge her.

Nia high-fived her. "I know that's right."

Samone eyed Nia. "Are you drunk?"

Nia ignored Samone. "Time for the gifts!"

Nia clapped her hands and headed to the front of the private room at Ciao Bella, the Italian eatery that she had rented out for the bridal brunch.

Nasi turned to Samone and asked, "Is it just me, or has Nia been acting weird all week?"

"Chile, you ain't the only one," Samone mumbled and then went to help Nia set up the chair that they had decorated for Nasi to sit in.

Instead of Nasi being a concerned friend, she automatically assumed that Nia was jealous of her for being the first one in the trio to marry, when in all actuality that was far from the case.

An hour or so later, Nasi had opened several gifts, some of which had brought the biggest smile to her face, and others of which had her wondering if her family really knew her, considering that Nasi hated candles and the other weird shit that she had received.

"Okay. It's my turn," Nia said cheerfully, clapping her hands together.

Samone had no idea what Nia had got Nasi. The only thing Samone had purchased was a few pieces from La Perla, a lingerie boutique in downtown New York.

Nia stepped off the small stage and left the private room. She returned with what looked like a statue of some sort, covered in a velvet black drape. She struggled to hold up the mannequin and balance herself in the stilettos she wore today.

Nia addressed the crowd as she held up the mannequin. "Okay, so before I unveil my gift, I just want to tell a little story about how I met Nasi."

She turned to her best friend and took a deep breath, not wanting to get emotional. "So, for those that don't know, I have a boutique at Third and Casper. I'll never forget that day. It was probably my first or second month in business, and things were so slow, but I was determined to make it. So, one night I was getting ready to close, and lo and behold, here comes Nasi, banging on the window, asking if I am closed. Of course, I told her we were closed. She insisted that I let her in, because she needed something to wear to a game, because a guy she was dating had invited her. So, long story made short, from that night on, she didn't just become my game buddy, but my friend, my sister, my confidante."

Nia took another deep breath before she continued. "Nasi, I consider it an honor to stand behind you on your special day. Samone and I are prepared to deal with Bridezilla." She laughed and wiped a lone tear from her face.

Nasi instantly began to regret that she had assumed that her best friend was jealous, especially since the thought had never crossed her mind before in the four years they had been friends. In fact, her sour-faced-ass sisters felt some type of way about her getting married, but not Nia.

"I love you, bitch. Now show me what you got me," Nasi said, then laughed, wiping tears from her face.

Nia turned the mannequin around and took the velvet drape off slowly, careful not to damage her masterpiece.

Everyone gasped, oohed, and aahed when they saw the wedding dress.

"Now, if you already had a dress in mind, then I promise you I under—" Nia began, wanting to explain herself in advance, but Nasi hushed her up.

"Nia . . . it's what I always imagined," she told her truthfully.

Nasi stood up and walked over to the dress and eyed it carefully, taking in the fabric, the train, the sleeves, the veil, and the corset. The dress was perfect and had truly been designed with Nasi in mind.

"Can I fit into this?" Nasi asked seriously.

Samone laughed. "Girl, I'm sure you can."

Nia reassured her. "You know I know your measurements to a tee."

It was nothing for Nia to whip Nasi something up in a matter of minutes if she had nothing to wear.

"This is the best gift ever, Nia!" Nasi hugged her friend. There weren't any words she could put together to describe her gratitude.

Today was what Nia had needed. Outside of work, she had been slowly drowning in her misery. She had been trying to stay afloat, because she had a business that had to keep going no matter what was going on in her personal life.

"I'm happy to hear that," Nia whispered into her best friend's ear, meaning every word.

If she couldn't be happy right now, the least she could do was put a smile on her friend's face.

The sound of the money-counter machine was the only thing that could be heard throughout the small house. East stood near the fireplace, with his arms crossed, his jaw flexed as he chewed on a stick of gum. He was irritated and tired. Hours of staying awake and making sure business was straightened out and taken care of, since the first of the month was nearing, had him ready to dive deep under the covers and catch up on some sleep. His eyes were bloodshot red, but he dared not complain. This was what he had wanted his whole life.

East was slowly building an empire, and he was doing it on his own, getting it straight from the gutter, with no handouts. So he knew, as sleepy as he was, he wasn't going anywhere any time soon.

"Phone up, baby girl," he called out to one of the chicks he had at a folding table, dividing the money.

He had been watching her ass carefully for the past ten minutes. She was fidgety and kept checking her cell phone, as if she had somewhere to be.

"I'm sorry," she said in a panicked tone. She turned and looked at East with tears in her eyes.

"What are you crying for?" He was confused, so he had genuinely asked her what was wrong.

She moved back from the table. "I have to get my kids, and no one is texting me back to go get them for me. They can't stay after school anymore," she cried.

East let out a breath of frustration. This was why he hated to deal with baby mamas, parents, anybody with extra responsibilities. "Okay, go," he told her, not wanting to see her cry anymore.

It wasn't that he had a weak spot for emotional women. The fact was, he considered her a distraction to the entire operation. With her ass crying and complaining, he couldn't focus on watching everybody else in the living room.

His henchmen were posted throughout the house, but East never left his post near the fireplace. Not only did he have a nine-millimeter handgun in the back of his pants, but he also had a gun strapped to his ankle, and there was a rifle lying across the mantel. The man wasn't playing any games about his money.

"I need the money, though," she pleaded.

East shrugged his shoulders. "You knew today was coming yesterday. Gotta be more prepared," he told her nonchalantly.

The girl gathered the few things she had come with, a bottle of Sprite, her cell phone and charger, and a small black bag of junk food to last her throughout the long day. East walked over to a pile of neatly stacked hundred-dollar bills and handed her three.

"Check her on the way out," he told Kevin, one of the dudes who worked for him.

East's phone rang, and he checked the screen, wishing it was Nia calling him to see what the plans were for tonight, but instead, it was some local bitch who still hadn't caught the hint that what they had was nothing more than that one night he fucked her. She had been texting him day in and day out, hinting around about making reservations, sending him pictures of shoes and bags that she wanted, and doing all kinds of other shit that East had no interest in.

He would never spend money on a girl he was just fucking. Nia was one of the few women who had enjoyed his time, his money, and his attention. She had deserved it, though, and if things were different, then she would still be his leading lady. However, as a man, he could not lie beside her every night with a heavy heart.

As much as it pained him to cut her off by distancing himself, it had to be done.

While they were no longer together, this didn't stop East from double tapping all her pictures and driving by her design studio just to make sure another nigga wasn't dropping her lunch off or doing all the simple shit he used to do for her.

East took pride in having been that special person for whom she put work aside so that they could have lunch together or catch a movie in the middle of the day.

If he could see her for only a few hours, it would make his day. Things had not been the same since she told him about her involvement with Biggs. East had thrown himself into the streets and had been traveling out of town to set up shop in the smallest towns. Wherever there was a lack of product, East was there, selling weed and any other drug at a discounted price. Not only did he have his hand in drug dealing, but recently he had begun to scam checks and sell guns too, and he was now interested in doing murder for hire.

The money he was chasing wasn't necessary. He was just doing anything he could to keep his mind from wandering. East didn't like being home anymore, because Nia had slowly left her touch there. From the new comforter she had purchased to the burnt-orange curtains she had sewn for his living room, Nia's presence was felt whenever he was at the crib.

"You good?" Harlem asked his friend, noticing that he appeared to be zoned out.

East really wasn't fucking with him like that, and he knew how to keep business and personal separate. Therefore, he kept his private challenges to himself.

"Yeah. I'm hungry, though." East rubbed his growling stomach.

Harlem was hungry too. "I'm going to send one of these bitches to go get some pizza or something," he told East.

Harlem's phone began to ring. His girlfriend, Chelle, had called three times in a row, so Harlem finally answered the phone. "Ma, I told you today was a busy day," he told her, growing irritated with her constant checking up on him.

She didn't do this because she was genuinely concerned about Harlem's well-being. Chelle wanted only to make sure he wasn't laid up with another ho while she was at home, waiting patiently for him to return.

Harlem's face relaxed once his girl told him why she had called. East figured they had something personal going on, so he walked away from Harlem and went into the kitchen to check on the crew that was posted at the dining-room table, cleaning guns.

"Everything good in here?" he asked.

Everyone nodded their head. They were all focused on making sure that there weren't any handprints on the guns and that they were cleaned correctly, so they could go. Everyone in the house had been working since yesterday without many breaks.

East would sit down and help every few hours, but because they were each getting paid one hundred dollars an hour, he planned to make sure they earned their pay.

"Yo," Harlem called out as he meandered through the house.

East knew he was probably looking for him, so he went back to the front of the house to see what he wanted.

"Yeah?" he said when he ran into Harlem. Then he waited on Harlem to say something.

"I know you and Nia were kicking it—" Harlem began, but East cut him off.

"Okay. And what?" he muttered, wondering what the fuck Harlem was about to say and why was he talking so slow.

Harlem looked down at his iPhone. "Chelle called and said Nia passed out or something. It's all on Instagram. She passed out in the mall, or something like that."

East didn't wait for anything else to come out of Harlem's mouth. He dashed out the door in less than 2.5 seconds and was down the street and on the highway in no time.

As he drove, he called the design studio and asked Kate for specific details, the most important being whether Nia was okay and which hospital was treating her. Because Kate was unaware that they had broken up—despite Nia's dark mood the past few weeks—she gave East the details. Never had she seen her boss openly admire someone the way she did East, so she felt perfectly comfortable giving him the information he was seeking. Kate wasn't blind to love, either, and she knew that without a doubt those two were meant to be together, even if things were shaky right now.

East didn't personally know any of Nia's friends—they hadn't got around to formal introductions—but she had spoken about them often. Kate had left East's name at the front desk, so after he reached the hospital, the receptionist escorted him to a private lobby. Thankfully, the hospital wasn't filled with tons of cameras and reporters.

"East!"

East looked around the private lobby for the person who had called his name. It was Kate.

Kate walked over to him and placed a hand on his shoulder.

"Is she okay?" he asked.

He wasn't the most spiritual person, but during the drive over, East had been silent and deep in thought, asking God to keep His hands on her.

"The doctor left right before you walked in. She said that Nia's fine. It was stress," Kate told him.

He took a deep breath, wanting to praise God that she was going to be okay, but he kept his cool and took a seat.

Samone and Nasi sat in a corner of the private lobby, wondering who the mysterious, handsome, tall dude covered in ink was and why he was asking questions about their best friend.

"Is that the guy they had been spotting her with on Media Take Out?" Nasi whispered to Samone.

Samone shrugged her shoulders. As far as she knew, Nia was not in a relationship. Nasi knew that Nia had been dating someone, but she didn't think it was that serious.

Nasi called Kate over to see who the guy was.

"That's Ms. Hudson's boyfriend," Kate told them matter-of-factly.

"Boyfriend!" Samone shouted, forgetting that there were other people in the lobby.

Harlem had just called East to get an update on Nia. They both couldn't be at the hospital. Someone had to watch them scandalous hoes who were counting the money. East stepped out to talk to Harlem.

"Well, hell, my friend did good, because he is fine," Nasi said proudly. She then turned to Samone and asked, "Why didn't she tell us she had a man?"

Samone wasn't sure how to answer her question, but a few things now made sense. This year Nia had gone from boring granny to happy girl back to boring granny. Her sudden mood changes were surprising, and even though Nia slipped back into her quiet and reserved persona, Samone was worried about her friend.

A nurse came out to get two of the ten guests waiting in the lobby for Nia. "Okay, people. Two at a time," she announced.

Nia considered her staff her family, and so were her two best friends. No one had bothered to call her aunt and cousin, because no one knew them. Nia had never talked about her blood family, and no one had brought the subject up, either.

"So, bitch, who's the cutie in the lobby, looking like he just lost his best friend?" Nasi asked Nia as soon as she and Samone walked into her hospital room.

Nia was groggy from the fall, but she was okay.

"Huh?" she whispered.

Samone laughed. She and Nasi thought their friend was being dramatic, but in truth, her head was pounding, and she didn't feel well.

"Don't play, boo-boo. Who is the guy outside?" Nasi placed her hands on her waist, wanting an answer.

East? Nia thought to herself.

"East is here?" she whispered.

That was the only person who crossed her mind. She wasn't talking to any other guy, and before East, she hadn't taken anyone seriously enough for them to stop what they were doing and run to her bedside.

The doctor had advised that she take it slow and not return to work for two weeks. But it wasn't like she'd been involved in a traffic accident. She fell at the mall because she hadn't eaten in a few days and had grown light-headed.

"Over my dead body," she'd mumbled to the doctor.

He had then warned her that she would be dead if she didn't slow down and start to relax.

"East. So that's his name. Yes, honey, he is here. He looks so sad, girl." Nasi went on and on. "Where did y'all meet? How long have y'all been talking?" she asked, bombarding Nia with questions.

Nia covered her face with her hands. She had always been a private person before the green light was shone on her life. "Get out," she whined.

Samone laughed, knowing how Nia hated to disclose her personal feelings and business.

"Oh, heffa, you just want us to leave so your boo can come back in here, but it's cool. We are happy you are doing better. How long do you have to stay here?" Nasi said, deciding to leave her friend alone.

Samone brushed Nia's hair back. Homegirl was looking a li'l rough.

"I don't know," she told them.

"Well, call or text if you need us to come back up here and get you," Samone told her.

"If East ain't playing doctor," Nasi teased.

Nia slowly shot her a middle finger. "Bye," she said.

They both kissed her forehead and made her promise to call. Then they left her room.

A soft knock on the door ten minutes later caused Nia to lift her head.

"Come in," she said with as much might as she could muster.

When East appeared before her, she looked in his eyes, but she didn't know what to say. Early on, she would steer her eyes away from his or drop her head, but as she spent more time with East, she grew comfortable in his presence and looked directly in his eyes. He still took her breath away.

He stared at her, not liking what he saw. Nia had lost a few pounds, dark circles had formed under her eyes, and she looked so tired.

"What's going on with you?" he asked in a scolding tone. He didn't mean for it to come out that way.

She lay back in the bed and said, "Working. You know me."

He crossed his arms and shook his head. "You'll learn to live one day," he told her.

Nia asked, "East, what are you doing here?"

She was happy to see him. It had been way too long, but the way he had left her . . . She did not appreciate it all.

"You know how much I care about you, so don't even ask me that shit," he told her, getting aggravated.

She sat up in bed and snorted. "You *care*? Do you really? I can remember a few nights I stayed up telling you how stressed I was and how you were my vacation from work."

She knew that East wasn't the one to blame for the fall, but he was the reason why she had been working so hard.

"Oh, it's my fault your ass doesn't know how to go home at a decent hour instead of working until the sun comes up?" he asked, just to make sure he had heard her correctly.

"You left me!" she shouted.

Now Nia was pissed. The heartbeat monitor went faster, and East saw it.

"All right, all right, Mama. Calm down," he urged, his tone softer, and he stepped closer to her bed and pushed her back gently toward the pillow, wanting her to get some sleep.

He knew she needed rest.

"You left," she repeated, wanting to hurt his feelings as much as he had hurt hers.

"I know, Ma," he admitted.

East hadn't expected Nia to go off on him like that, and deep down inside, it felt good to hear her trip out on him.

Nia yawned. She would be asleep any second now. The medicine had finally kicked in.

"Where are you going?" she asked him.

"Nowhere, bae. Go to sleep."

He walked around her bed and sat on the small blue couch against the wall.

"Okay," Nia said, giving in. She closed her eyes and was knocked out and snoring in minutes.

East made a few plays from his trap phone before getting up to go see what the cafeteria had. If he didn't eat something soon, he too would be falling out. When he got back to Nia's room with a Chick-fil-A bag, Nia was up, and she had visitors in the room.

"I'll come back," he told her.

She shook her head. "No. East, this is my attorney, my business manager, and my publicist. Everyone, this is my boyfriend," she said without much hesitation.

East didn't correct her, but he was surprised that she still felt as if he deserved that title.

"Hello," they all said in different ways.

After the meeting ended and Nia's publicist had been given the green light to release a public statement about her condition, the three visitors there on business were all out the door.

"I'm hungry," she told East once they were alone. He was sitting in the chair next to her bed.

"Can you eat?" he asked, not wanting to give her a sandwich if she wasn't supposed to have it.

She shrugged her shoulders. "Why would I not be able to? I'm not sick," she reminded him.

East got up and handed her one of the two sandwiches he'd bought. "You want some ketchup?" he asked.

Nia told him no and ripped open the sandwich bag. She was more than ready to eat.

"So, I'm still your boyfriend?" East asked, popping a serious question.

She rolled her eyes. "You tell me."

It was not Nia who had flipped the script and changed things between them; it was East.

"There's a lot you don't know about me," he told her, giving her a forewarning.

Nia was good shit. Her head was on her shoulders. She had goals, dreams, and ambition. East had those things too, but they were on two different paths, though they both were chasing the same thing. He never wanted to be a bad influence in her life or the reason she didn't reach her full potential.

A nigga like East was grateful to see another birthday. Nia was a planner; he wasn't.

Between the two of them, magic had been created. Together, they were perfect. Where she fell short, he picked up the slack. Nia shared her business insight with East, and in return, he told her how to break her money down and divide it equally among her business ventures. Nia had faith and determination, and they slowly showered down on East. They benefited each other, and despite his background and his current career choice, Nia still wanted to be with him.

"And I still want to be with you, so what does that tell you, East?" she asked, not backing down anymore.

Nia refused to run from love, happiness, and joy. East brought her those three things, and she desperately needed him back in her life. She was tired of feeling incomplete.

He ran his hands over her face and looked into her beautiful eyes.

Harlem's words about him pursuing Nia replayed in his mind. *Not her, man, not her.*

But what the fuck did Harlem know?

No one but the two of them knew how they made each other feel.

"I want to be with you too, shorty. You know that," he said.

She heard the hesitation in his voice. He was holding back with her. Nia wanted to be with him. She was prepared to go all in, no brakes.

However, she refused to do it alone. If they weren't on the same page, then she would continue to do her, with the hope that God would send her the man who was designed for her. She wouldn't give East a presentation of her accolades and such to convince him to be with her.

It was either a yes or a no.

She patiently waited on him to continue, but it seemed as if he had nothing else to say.

"Now what?" she asked, growing irritated with him playing games.

He laughed. "I know you miss the dick. I see the hunger in your eyes, Ma."

Nia hugged East from the back. They were standing outside, on the balcony of their vacation cottage, which had a breathtaking view of their island paradise, which was not too far from Buenos Aires, Argentina. This was her first vacation where no work was involved. She had surprised herself when she packed a multitude of bikinis but no undergarments, as East had insisted. So far, he was right.

From morning to night, the only activity the couple engaged in was sex, that is, until today. Nia hadn't had this much sex in her life.

When the doctor had told East that she needed to relax and not think about anything that involved hassles, he had come up with the perfect strategy. They would take that vacation they'd spoken about. He had asked her where she wanted unwind, and without much hesitation, Nia had told him. He was thankful that Nia had connections and could arrange chartered flights and shit.

Today was the first day they had left the small yet cozy and romantic cottage, and their day had been full of fun.

Nia and East had gone on some of the tours the island offered. It was his first time scuba diving and deep-sea fishing, and he had had fun and would definitely do it again. Nia's secret obsession was photography, so she had spent the day snapping candid photos of herself and her lover on the beach.

The sun was slowly falling, as Nia now hugged East out on the balcony. Before she joined him, East had been outside having a drink and smoking a hand-rolled cigar that he picked up in the village on the walk back to their residence.

"How was your shower?" he asked her.

"Perfect. I'm surprised you didn't join me." She reached up on her tippy toes and kissed the back of his neck.

East pulled her around in front of him, and they traded places. She now leaned against the railing, and he hovered behind her, smoking and sipping.

"I'm giving you a break," he told her, pinching her side.

"Thank you," she told him playfully.

However, if he asked her to undress and bend over right now, she would oblige.

East nuzzled her neck and planted soft kisses on her collarbone. "You smell so good," he told her.

Both of them had needed this vacation, not because their jobs were demanding, but to reestablish their connection. Surprisingly, they had gotten back together easily, as if they'd been separated only for days, not weeks. Nia had not brought up the tears and the feelings of depression and sadness she'd endured while they were apart. She had spoken of nothing but happiness, because that was what she was experiencing now.

Too scared to ruin a perfect day, she kept her questions to herself for now. But soon she would ask him, "What do you want and expect out of a relationship?" It was vital to her that they stayed on the same page, since it seemed as if not doing so was how they had wavered in the first place. She wanted East to trust her and vice versa.

The way he had been fucking her made her think he hadn't shared his bed with other women during her absence, and he hadn't. East had engaged in sex, but he hadn't dared bring another bitch into the home that he shared openly with Nia.

"Am I it for you?" he asked, as if reading her mind.

She smiled at the timing of his question. It was crazy how they both had the same fears about their love, she thought. She blushed at his nervous antics.

Nia turned around and draped her arms around his neck. "Am I it for you?" she asked, posing the same question.

East tilted his head and gave her that bad-boy look that she was slowly falling in love with. "You already know," he told her straight up.

She shook her head. "Well, what made you ask me, then?" she questioned, because she felt the same way.

He didn't want to seem so insecure, but he couldn't help but feel that way. Nia was a prized possession. She was a rare gem, a queen, a goddess, an angel and, most importantly, his quiet in the middle of a storm. East knew niggas wanted her. He had seen the thirst comments and the constant woman crush Wednesday posts on his timeline.

"I don't have groupies." He winked in an attempt to play things cool.

Nia thought it was cute that he was jealous. "I'll be your groupie, baby," she sang to him.

"I'm serious, babe," he told her, wanting to keep her focused on the conversation.

She sighed and dropped her arms from around his neck and turned back around to look at the view again, not wanting to miss the sun going down.

"It's me and you, as long as you'll have me," she told him.

East came closer and kissed the side of her neck again. "All right. I'll take that," he said.

"Until I give you a reason to question me, don't," Nia stated firmly.

East could only respect that. "One hundred."

After he finished his cigar, they grabbed their shoes and walked down the beach to have a candlelight dinner.

They were escorted to their table right away, and East ordered a bottle of champagne.

"What we toasting to?" Nia asked after the waiter appeared with the champagne, popped the cork on the bottle, and poured.

"To getting this motherfucking money," he said happily, a tad bit anxious to return to the streets.

Nia cut her eyes at him.

He erupted in laughter. "And to us too, babe," he added, knowing she hated when he talked that way.

"And to more trips," she added happily.

"*Saluti*," East said, mocking an Italian, as he lifted his flute.

The man had watched *The Godfather* one too many times.

After they finished their meal of grilled rainbow trout and grilled vegetables, East led Nia farther down the beach.

"All right, boo. We already on a private island. We need to stay where the lights are," she warned.

East said, "Man, I'ma shoot the shit out of a nigga if they try some shit."

"You got your gun?" She didn't even know he packed one.

"I don't go nowhere without my gun," he told her.

Nia thought of Biggs for a second, remembered he was the same way, and still someone had caught him slipping.

"Come here." He pulled her closer to him.

Ahead of them, she saw a trail of lights and heard a guitar and also what sounded like drums or a banjo. "Where are we?"

"You probably don't even remember the day you told me that you dance only when you're out of town, because it's when you feel free and you don't having to worry about nobody watching you," he said.

Nia's heart skipped a beat. The couple had discussed so many different things over the past few months. She could only imagine what else she had told him that she didn't remember right now, but with a few glasses of wine, she was sure she had revealed some more crazy secrets. East remembering that one simple detail meant more to her than he would ever know.

"Sooo, are you telling me we're about to dance?" she asked.

He laughed and twirled her around. "You're going to dance, and I'm going to get high and watch," he said.

Once they joined the small group of people who were playing music, making drinks, and dancing, it took only two shots of the local rum for Nia to unwind. She had already downed three glasses of champagne over dinner and had puffed a few times on East's blunt. She was feeling real wavy.

"Work them hips, girl," East said, encouraging her.

Nia threw her head back in laughter. She danced with the locals and learned a few new dance moves. She was truly having the time of her life.

At one point, Nia dropped down low, doing some dance she had made up, and blew a kiss in East's direction.

He mouthed three special words, "I love you," unable to keep his thoughts to himself any longer.

She froze on the way up from dancing down to the ground and stared at him.

He smiled and puffed on the blunt.

East was tipsy too, but he meant what he'd said. He loved her with everything in him, and regardless of how Harlem or any other nigga felt, Nia was his. Fuck whoever came before him, including that nigga Biggs.

9

"They don't wanna see me love you."

– Kanye West

Friday nights were normally reserved for a glass of wine and a recap of all the television shows that she had missed, but whenever Nasi sent a text to the group, asking if her two close friends would accompany her to a basketball game, Nia always told her yes.

Basketball games in New York were like a fashion show. Of course, the game was going on, and people went to watch the sport, but the women didn't. Basketball wives, girlfriends, groupies, and mistresses all spent the week preparing for that one night. The games had four quarters, but halftime was the focal point. It was a crazy situation.

This Friday night was one of those basketball nights for the three friends. As they sat in their seats at Madison Square Garden, Nasi checked her makeup for the fifth time in the past ten minutes and asked Nia for the second time, "Do you like what I have on?"

Samone answered for her. "Girl, yes! Why the fuck you keep asking her that? If you didn't want to wear that tight-ass dress, then you shouldn't have worn it."

Nia bit down on her bottom lip, unsure of what to say. She, too, was confused as to why Nasi was so dressed up. Instead of looking like the wholesome and humble fiancée that she truly was, she had on a face full of makeup that didn't match her complexion and a leather minidress that had all her business on Front Street. Her cleavage spilled out it.

Normally, Nia would style Nasi for the games, but for the past two weeks Nasi had been using a new stylist. Since Nia was a very busy woman, she wasn't bothered at all by Nasi's defection.

Tonight she had donned a gray, knee-length dress and silver Givenchy sandals. See, Nia was one of those "It doesn't take much" girls. She'd paired her outfit with a fox fur vest and a rose-gold teardrop-diamond pendant necklace. She wore no makeup and no earrings and had her hair pushed back into a low ponytail at the nape of her neck.

For various reasons, Nia hadn't dressed up or got her face done today. She knew she wasn't going out after the game, and she had had a long day. Besides, she hadn't known until the last minute that she would be attending this game. Nasi had texted her and Samone two hours before the game, letting them know that she had lucked upon two extra tickets.

"Mone, today is not the fucking day," Nasi snapped under her breath, careful not to attract too much attention.

Even when everyone else appeared to be focused on the game, they really were not.

Samone could only chuckle at how lost her friend was slowly becoming. She didn't understand why Nasi always tried so hard. For instance, Nia looked like she had come straight from work, and so did Samone, who wore a pair of fitted jeans and an oversize T-shirt with a black fedora hat.

Growing up in a family where money was never really an issue, Samone had learned that *wealth* was quiet and *rich* was loud and flashy. Tonight Nasi was screaming green dollar bills. Samone knew that her friend was going through some things, but if Nasi didn't share them openly with her, then Samone wouldn't beg to know her business.

"Okay, ladies, let's chill and have another drink, shall we?" Nia said, smiling, and stood to her feet. "I'll get us all a round of shots." Then she headed to the bar.

Samone had noticed that her friend was smiling again, and she was sure that the credit went to her new love interest.

Nia stood in the long line at the bar, waiting her turn to order a round of shots. She bobbed her head to the music blaring from the speakers.

"Nia . . . Nia Hudson?" Someone was calling her name.

She prayed it wasn't anyone whose calls she had been dodging. Since she and East had returned from the islands, she had been taking things easy. She had been delegating more tasks to her staff and had been going home early, and she'd started working out and dieting again. Nia refused to be dead before the age of fifty because she didn't know how to manage her schedule and delegate tasks. Gone were the days of her hustling for a buck. Nia had reached a pivotal point in her career, and it was time for her to start celebrating life and her accomplishments.

Nia looked around and saw a woman rushing her way. It was Marisol, an associate from her past. "Hey, girl! Oh my God! How have you been?" Nia exclaimed when Marisol came to a halt before her. She and Marisol had worked together back in the day. Nia would never forget the good ole days of interning during Fashion Week.

"Girl, I've been great. I can't believe I ran into you tonight. I was just asking around for your direct contact info. You're a hard lady to get in contact with," Marisol told her.

Nia chuckled, knowing she was telling the truth, but she always told people, "If you really want to get in contact with me, you'll leave a message with the receptionist at my design studio." The majority of her time was spent at that one place. Nia hosted events, styled clients, sewed wedding dresses, and even held meetings at the design studio. Most people knew where to find her, so apparently, Marisol hadn't been looking hard enough.

"How can I help you?" Nia asked as she moved up in the long line at the bar.

Marisol fumbled with her phone. She wanted to show Nia a visual. "So, I'm putting together a fashion show with several designers. The money goes to Mexico, for building a school and a few other things," she told her.

Nia donated enough money throughout the year, and her time as well.

"Can you send this to my publicist?" she asked Marisol.

It was a Friday night, and she wasn't in the mood to discuss business or money at a basketball game. Nia wanted to enjoy the game with her girls, then go home to her man, who she had been missing all day.

"Sure, sure. Let me get the e-mail."

Nia recited the e-mail and then told her, "I'll get in touch with you through her. Good seeing you." She ended the conversation and ordered a round of Patrón shots.

"Damn, girl. What took you so long? We could have ordered with the waitress," Nasi fussed once Nia made it back to her seat.

She ignored her homegirl, handed out the shots of Patrón, and tossed hers back.

"Ooh-wee," Samone said, teasing Nia.

Nia wasn't much of a shot taker. Everyone knew Nia loved her wine.

Nasi straightened her posture once she saw Harry making his way down the court, dribbling the ball with his left hand.

Nia noticed her friend's sudden movement, and she had to ask, "Is everything okay with y'all?"

It wasn't like Nia to prod into other people's business, but lately something had been off with Nasi. Nia knew that she and East had been spending a lot of quality time together, but Nia would never put a man before the well-being of her friends.

Nasi smiled at her friend and wagged her ring finger and said, "Why would it not be? I'm engaged."

Samone damn near choked on the nachos she was eating. "Since when did a ring buy happiness?" she asked Nasi.

Nia was thinking the same thing, but she wouldn't say anything to cause a scene.

"I n-never said it did. I am simply saying, Why wouldn't things be okay with us? We're getting married," Nasi stammered.

"Okay, girl." Samone let the conversation go, because Nasi was tripping, and it was very obvious.

The game came to an end, and the New York Knicks won by twenty points.

"We gotta go celebrate. Where y'all wanna go?" Nasi said.

Nia yawned, and Samone said, "I have a session with Mark Brady tonight."

Samone was the hottest tattoo artist in her industry, and celebrities would either fly her to their home or fly into the city for a private session with Samone. When the money called, going out and not doing any shit but standing around and staring at strangers had to hit the back burner. She was about to go home and squeeze in a nap before it was time for her to open the shop up for Mark and his friends.

"Boo-hoo. All right. Catch you later," Nasi said. "What about you, Nia?" she asked her other friend.

Nia really didn't want to go anywhere, but she hadn't heard from East since earlier in the day. Therefore, it wasn't guaranteed that they would be laid up tonight, anyway.

"I'll go, but not for long, Nasi. Only a few hours," Nia told her, and she made sure they made direct eye contact so Nasi would know that she was serious.

"Yayyy! Turn up! Okay, let me see what the other wives are doing tonight," Nasi said before walking off.

Samone hissed, "Something ain't right, Nia."

Nia agreed. "Yeah, but she'll tell us when she wants to. Be safe tonight, girl. Send pictures," she told her friend before giving her a warm hug.

"You're glowing," Samone said, commenting on Nia's rosy cheeks.

Nia played it off, not wanting to say too much right now. She and East were a delicate topic for her.

"Something like that." Nia made a so-so motion with her hand.

Samone knew how her friend was, so she didn't press the topic. "Let me know when you get in the house," she said and then proceeded toward the exit.

Nia sat down and texted East while she waited on Nasi. Going out tonight, love, she texted.

East responded minutes later with one word, and that was *cool*. She figured he was busy, so she ended the conversation there.

Nasi returned just then. "Okay, girlie. Let's go to my house to pregame."

Nia was cool with that, so she followed Nasi to the private parking lot where the players and their families parked their vehicles.

"You caught an Uber?" Nasi asked once they had pulled out of the parking lot and were stuck in the game traffic.

"Girl, you know I don't drive in this mess," Nia reminded her.

Nasi turned the radio on and danced around in her seat. She was so happy that the Knicks had won the game tonight, and that Harry had racked up twenty-two points tonight, which meant he would be in a great mood for the next few days. As much as she loved basketball season and attending all the home games, her fiancé was so moody, and she could never predict his attitude. She was counting down until the play-offs and, hopefully, the championship. After that, Harry would have a few months to relax, and Nasi had already begun to plan their vacations. Her honey had been working so hard to stay on top of his game, and she wanted him to unwind on a few different private beaches.

"Where are we going tonight?" Nia asked once they had tossed back a few more shots back at Nasi's condo.

Nasi told her they were hitting up a new club that the team had been invited to tonight. Just then the front door opened and closed, and Nasi's face lit up once she realized her fiancé was now home.

"I'll be back," she told Nia and ran off to the foyer, screaming, "Baby!"

Nia laughed at how cute her friend was. She prayed that she and East still felt that way years later.

"Man, what the fuck you got on?" Nia jumped when she heard Harry shouting at her friend.

Nasi hushed him. "Nia is here," she told him quickly, not wanting him to embarrass her in front of Nia.

"What is she here for? Your man won the game, and you got company," he snapped.

Nia shook her head and slipped her feet back into her heels. She had already pulled up the Uber app on her phone.

Minutes later, Nasi returned to the living room, and Nia didn't give her a chance to make up an excuse as to why they weren't going out.

"Girl, something came up. I have to get going," Nia told her.

Nasi looked so sad and pitiful, and Nia wondered what was really going on with her best friend.

"Okay, girl. Harry is tired, anyway, so I'm about to cook and get in the bed."

Nia wanted to say, "Cook? Girl, it's eleven o'clock at night," but that was not her business.

Instead she said, "Call me tomorrow." She kissed Nasi's cheek and showed herself out of the penthouse condo.

She took the elevator down thirty-nine floors and waited in the lobby on her Uber. It didn't take her long to get home, because she and Nasi didn't live too far away from each other.

Once Nia was home, she undressed, bathed, and slipped on one of East's T-shirts. She missed her beau and wished he was there with her, rubbing her thighs as they watched a movie on television, but she knew how crazy his schedule was on the weekends. Nia cuddled on the couch alone and kicked back with a glass of wine, the bottle not too far away.

Her phone vibrated as soon as she pressed PLAY on season three, episode two, of a television show that she was binge-watching on Netflix. The time on her phone read 3:53 a.m. She knew that only one person would be calling her at this hour.

"You're outside?" she asked when she answered the phone, already knowing the routine.

"Yep, boo. Buzz me up," he said coolly.

Nia smiled at the sound of his voice. The minutes could not go by fast enough. She stood by the door, waiting on him to walk in.

"Why you out of the bed?" he asked once he had walked in and locked the door.

Nia did not even respond. She bum-rushed him and planted kisses on his face.

"Damn," he mumbled as his hands became reacquainted with her body, although it had not been that long since the last time he entered her and made sweet love to his woman.

"I missed you," she whispered in his ear as she slowly wrapped her tongue around his earlobe.

It was one of his soft spots, and Nia knew that. She went back to kissing his neck as she fumbled with his belt buckle.

"Take 'em off," she commanded.

"You drunk, boo?" East asked and laughed as he did what she had told him to do.

Nia yawned. As sleepy as she was, she still wanted some dick.

Once they both were buck naked, Nia dropped to her knees and began to bless him.

After a long day of doing all kinds of illegal shit, he considered it a relief to come home, lean his body against the wall, and have his queen suck his problems away. East allowed Nia to take his mind elsewhere. The bullshit in the streets—product being scarce, money not being right, and niggas folding—didn't matter right now. East would deal with the bullshit in the morning.

Right now, he wanted to make love to Nia, smoke a blunt, eat up whatever she had in the fridge, fuck her once more, and then fall asleep with his hands wrapped around her waist.

Nia gripped his dick using her lips. She was truly the best he had ever had in his life. It had taken him some time to train her mouth to suck his dick how he liked it, but baby girl had mastered the art perfectly.

"Yeah, yeah . . . slow like that, baby," he coached her.

Nia allowed him to run his hands through her hair. He fucked her face real slow. She began to gag, and East let out a guttural moan.

"Come here," he said.

He picked her ass up so fast and spun her around, then bent her over in the middle of the hallway. He kneeled behind her and kissed her left and right ass cheeks and then stuck his tongue in her ass while his fingers toyed with her pussy.

Nia's pussy began to sing to him.

"Hell yeah. Talk to me," he said loudly.

"Fuck me please," she begged, twerking her cheeks against his face.

East stood to his feet and smacked her ass before he inserted his penis into her from behind. He took a deep breath, tried his hardest not to moan out like a bitch, but with Nia, he could not help it. Not only did she fit him like a glove, but also her pussy made noises that drove him crazy. Literally.

"Yes," she said as she rocked back and forth, forcing East to get with the motion that she had going on.

Nia moved her hips and ass, and he held on to her waist, letting Li'l Mama do her. Nia struggled to stay upright. East was long stroking her so good that she was growing weak.

"I can't . . . ," she said in a low voice. He was fucking her into a coma. She couldn't think straight or talk.

He pulled her backward into the kitchen, then picked her up and sat her on the counter. Nia scooted as close to him as she could get, wanting to hug, kiss, and smell him. Everything about East caused her to feel intoxicated.

"I love you, baby," East told her over and over again as he fucked her pussy up.

Nia moaned in his ear before dropping her head over his shoulder. Her hair fell over his face. Her knees were shaking profusely, and she knew that she was about to erupt.

"I feel that pussy trying to cum on Daddy Dick. Let it rain, boo," he begged her.

She tried her hardest not to cum so prematurely, but the truth was, this wasn't her first or second time coming since East had first walked through the door. At the sight of him, her pussy had creamed.

"Shit!" she screamed when his dick was replaced with that hurricane tongue.

Nia had so many good things to say about East, and an important one was that sexually, he was such a giver. He cared about her getting hers off, and he wouldn't dare slow down or stop until he knew for a fact that he had drained every drop of cum out of her.

East drilled down on her clit and used his bottom lip to suck it harder, causing her to squirt across his nose and forehead.

"Hell, yeah!" He smacked his lips on her pussy, as if it was his last meal.

Nia couldn't see him jerking off his own dick as he ate her pussy, but East was going to work. Once he felt his own nut building up, he hopped up on the counter and ejaculated on her thigh.

"Shit," he said once he had squeezed out all the cum he had.

They both were so tired after that. They didn't even make it to the shower or the bed. Nia used the kitchen cloth to wipe them down, and then they laid their naked bodies on the couch, their limbs entangled. A few minutes later, East spread over them the blanket that was on the floor across them, and just like that, the couple was knocked out.

***

The next morning, Nia woke up first, unable to sleep as long as her boyfriend did. She bathed and went into her home office to get some work done.

With Nasi still on her mind, and Harry's rude outburst weighing on her, she shot her friend a text message, suggesting brunch or dinner tonight.

Nia didn't have long until it was time for her to head to the design studio and open the boutique. After double-checking with Kate about the DJ, bartender, and chef being on time today, she went to get dressed for work.

"Babe, call me later. Lock the bottom lock," Nia whispered in East's ear when she was ready to head out.

The only thing he did was mumble, "Okay," before turning his naked body over, exposing his brown ass, and going right back to snoring.

He was not an early bird at all, so she knew that he would not be up anytime soon. Nia straightened up a little before walking out the door.

Hours later, the boutique was in full swing, and it was safe to say that they would probably sell out of everything way before the store closed.

"Do we have any more of the emerald bangles in stock?" asked Desiree, one of Nia's seamstresses.

Nia was distracted, so instead of answering the question, she suggested to Desiree that it might be best if all the seamstresses dropped by to help out in the boutique at least once a month so that they could personally connect with clients and get a feel for what they were looking for. That way when the seamstresses had their team meetings, they would have fresh and bright designs to present. Although stylists, staff members, and seamstresses were not highly compensated for working in the boutique, Nia was certain they would reap greater rewards in the long run. She was preparing to expand her brand in the United States, and she was thinking about an international presence as well. That would make the company more profitable.

With those goals in mind, Nia had been carefully observing every person on her team. She knew she could not build the company alone. Her stress levels were still somewhat elevated, and her team had suggested that she appoint people whom she could trust and who had excellent leadership capabilities. And she needed her team's help to develop the company's creative potential.

"Whew." Nia found herself constantly yawning.

She didn't think last night's activity had worn her body out, but apparently it had. She was looking forward to cleaning up and shutting the design studio so she could go home and get back in the bed. She was turning into a lovestruck grandmother. Lovestruck because all her spare time was being spent with her boyfriend, and a grandmother because the only thing she could think about right now was her bed. Nia was now relieved that Nasi had read her message but hadn't responded, as Nia no longer had the energy to get together with her friend today. She planned on sleeping the rest of the weekend away and grabbing dinner with East tomorrow if he had time.

"Nia, do we have any more emerald bangles?" Desiree asked again.

"Sorry, girl. I heard you the first time. My mind is somewhere else today," she said, apologizing.

Desiree smiled and told her, "Trust me, I understand."

"I'll go get a few more," Nia said, and then she took the elevator up to the stockroom to grab the bangles.

When Nia returned, it seemed as if the number of people in the boutique had doubled.

"Oh my," she mumbled.

"Oh my, is right. We need a bigger building," one of her staff members said and laughed.

Nia had been thinking the same thing, but it would take away from the "rare pieces" concept, which was what she had built her brand on. It wasn't easy to get on Nia Hudson's design schedule, and she had promised herself when she first started that it would always stay that way.

Fifteen minutes later the bottom floor of the design studio was overflowing with all kinds of people, from A-list to C-list celebrities, locals shopping in the area, and fans of Nia to people who were visiting and wanted to stop by and take a picture at the now famous ND Studios. The only thing Nia could do was look up at the ceiling and thank God for blessing a little girl from Brooklyn with a special gift.

The crowd was a marvelous thing to behold, but today had been extremely long. As she worked, Nia began to count the days until her and East's next getaway. On the flight back to the States from Buenos Aires, he had made her promise to allow him to whisk her away every two months, and Nia was now looking forward to their next vacation.

"Please look like you want to be here," her publicist whispered in her ear after returning with a program.

Nia yawned and rubbed her right eye with the palm of her hand. "I'm trying," she whined.

Ever since she'd fallen down at the mall, Nia had been popping up at more fashion shows in New York.

Although Nia didn't care what most people said about her, a few blogs had said that she was getting washed up, and this had hurt her feelings. The sad thing was Nia hadn't even been in the game for ten years yet. She was five years shy of planting her feet firmly in this industry.

She had so much more up her sleeve to offer the fashion industry. Her lingerie line was under development, and her affordable workout gear was set to launch in Target stores nationwide. Nia was also in negotiations to start her home goods line. Being with East and cooking dinner about twice a week had inspired her to create a dishware line. Her brain never stopped working and generating new ideas and ways to produce income, so for a blogger to write that she was washed up, well, they had no idea what Nia Hudson had in store for the world.

She sat up in the uncomfortable wooden chair in the front row at the fashion show and crossed one long leg over the other. The yellow python pumps by Céline were fresh out of the box. It hadn't been twenty-four hours since these shoes were posted on the Céline Web site, and Nia Hudson had already been spotted wearing them.

She wore a white jumpsuit with a plunging sweetheart neckline and a sparkling diamond necklace, a gift from her man. East did not just spoil her with material things, but he also gave her his love, and his love had not faltered as time went on. In fact, it had grown more and more.

Things were going so perfectly. Sometimes Nia could hardly believe it, so she pinched him while he slept to make sure he wasn't a ghost.

"Who is she?" Nia asked Kate. Even though Kate was the receptionist at ND, lately, Nia had been inviting Kate along everywhere she went.

Kate was proving to be a workhorse in the design studio, arriving early and staying late. She knew Nia's schedule like the back of her hand, and she didn't mess up. Kate reminded Nia of herself. They were both perfectionists and were always striving for excellence.

Nia felt bad that she had promised her assistant that when she returned from maternity leave, she would still have her job, but this wasn't looking too promising these days. Kate was single and was anxious to learn all she could. Nia loved that shit about her and was considering making Kate her assistant.

Kate leaned over and whispered into her boss's ear, "That's Angel, an upcoming designer from Atlanta."

Nia nodded her head. She made a mental note to get the woman's contact information before she left. The way Angel's models posed at the end of the runway was different. Her designs were stylish, and Nia would love to talk to her about becoming a private sponsor for her line.

Nia gave back often to the fashion community. There were several successful designers and boutiques across the United States that had got that push they needed with the help of Nia's funds. She remembered staying up all night to work on designs and pawning clothes and other nice things she had in her possession to buy fabric and materials. Nia would never forget her beginnings and the struggle. She was a girl who had had nothing and now had everything. And she was committed to giving back. Her dreams had truly become her reality, and it felt so damn good to say to aspiring designers, "I made it, and you can, too!"

After the fashion show there was an after-party, and Nia had been paid twenty-five hundred dollars to make an appearance at it, so that that was where she went. She found her way to the club's private section, towing along a few pretty girls she had personally pulled out of the long line out of the club. Nia found her table, which was laden with food and drink, and took a seat. She knew she wouldn't be able to drink four bottles of Cîroc herself or eat all the food that the club had provided, so she told the girls to have a seat and enjoy themselves.

Meanwhile Kate stood near the rope just outside the club. She had invited along her little sister, who was in town visiting, and was waiting on her to enter the club.

Nia bobbed her head to the tunes of Eryn Allen Kane, one of her new favorite people to jam to while getting ready. The DJ had mixed her song with a beat produced by Pharrell, so the club was vibing. Nia ran her hands over her hair to smooth the flyaways and then dropped her hands to her waist and rocked her shoulders and tapped her foot.

She was enjoying herself, even though she hadn't thought she would, considering she hadn't been in the mood to do anything tonight. East had just texted her and had told her he was coming across the bridge, so she stood to leave. Nia told the girls at her table to have fun and be safe.

"You're leaving?" Kate asked as she approached Nia's table. She wanted her to meet her sister, who had got lost in the main section of the club.

She nodded her head. "We have an early morning," Nia reminded her.

Kate would not be out long, either. "Yes, ma'am."

Nia kissed her cheek and held on to Kate's hand as she stepped down the stairs, leaving the VIP section and entering the crowded main section of the club. On her way out, she saw Harlem and Chelle, and a few other people that she didn't recognize. It would be rude if she didn't speak to Harlem and his girlfriend, so she made her way over to the bar where they stood.

"What y'all doing here?" she asked jokingly.

Harlem was a hood nigga all day every day. This posh and upscale club, which rarely played rap music, wasn't really his scene, so she knew he was there because his girlfriend was an aspiring designer.

"You know she dragged me out," Harlem said coolly.

Nia smiled and waved at Chelle. "Good seeing you again," she told her.

Chelle returned the gesture, then turned around and went back to turning up with her friends. Nia felt the shade, but she was grown and didn't entertain her at all.

Harlem commented on Nia's outfit. "Still fly," he said.

She dusted her shoulders playfully. "Hey, you know how I do."

"So, what's up with you and East?"

Harlem had never been one to beat around the bush. But she was taken aback by his forwardness.

"What you mean, what's up? We are good."

Nia was far from a dummy, and if being with Biggs didn't teach her anything else, it had taught her how to smell bullshit a mile away, and Harlem smelled funky.

"Shit. You with that nigga. How disrespectful is that?" he muttered.

It was time for her to go, before she lost her religion and her cool in such a public place.

"It was good seeing you. I'll tell East you said hello," she told him with malice in her voice, and then she walked off.

She asked one of the security guards to escort her to her car, and once there, she tipped him a twenty-dollar bill and peeled off.

When she made it to East's house, he was sleeping and snoring, so she kept tonight's conversation with Harlem to herself and went to shower before she joined him in bed. Nia wondered what had made Harlem come at her like that. Was dating East wrong?

She had never seen East around Biggs, so what was the problem? Did Harlem really expect her never to move on, or was he annoyed that she had moved on with his homie? Was that what the issue was?

Soon she succumbed to sleep, and the questions faded. She dreamed of wedding bells and babies.

Life was great, and loving East made it better.

10

"I dig your actions, but . . . I listen to the things you say."

— *Whitney Houston*

Love made Nia comfortable. She hadn't imagined that this day would come. East came into the room, holding a wooden tray. Atop the tray was a bowl of canned chicken noodle soup, crackers, a mug of tea with honey and squeezed lemon, and a heating pad that needed to be plugged in.

"Wake up, bae," East told his girlfriend. An hour or two ago, he had rubbed her soft feet until she fell asleep. His hands had to have been touched by God, because he gave the best massages.

"I'm up," she whined, rolling over and sitting up so she could put something in her stomach.

He turned the television on after he sat the tray on the bed. "You want the lights on?" he asked.

She shook her head and stuck a cracker in her mouth. It was that time of the month, and East had canceled his errands for today and was staying in with Nia to make sure she ate and got as much sleep as she could. It seemed as if every month her cramps worsened. Having grown up with two older sisters, he knew exactly what to do to make Li'l Mama feel better.

Nia had her cell phones on silent and had forwarded all her business e-mails to Kate. The only thing she had done for the better part of the day was watch movies and sleep on and off.

"Hmmm," she moaned after taking a sip of the chamomile tea.

"It's good?" he asked, but with the help of his grandmother, he was positive he had fixed it right.

Nia told him yes and sat the mug on the nightstand and rested her head against the pillow. "I feel like shit," she complained. She was impatiently waiting on the medicine to kick in.

"You'll feel better if you eat the soup, boo," East suggested, coming around to her side of the bed and lifting the bowl so he could feed her.

She smiled at her man trying to play nurse. He was such a sweetie, and Nia was thankful for him.

"What you smiling at me for?" he asked, blushing, because as sick as she was, and as disheveled as her appearance was right now, she still took his breath away.

Nia's hair was sloppily tied into a bun on the top of her head. She wore a pair of white Fendi reading glasses from when she was scanning the newest issue of *Vogue*. Nia had on one of East's T-shirts that he wore around the house, a pair of cotton panties, and black leggings.

"I'm smiling at your fine ass," she teased.

East scooped up a few noodles with the large spoon and told her to open up. She obeyed. After she had eaten half of the soup, East was sure she was good and full, so he removed the tray from the bed and plugged the heating pad into the wall.

"Where you want it?" he asked, standing over her with the heating pad.

She motioned to her belly, and he laid it across her midsection and pulled the comforter over her body and kissed her forehead.

"Anything else you need, baby?" he asked, wanting her to be as relaxed as possible.

She told him, "I'm good for now. Thanks for everything."

He rubbed the side of her face.

"Holler if you need me," East told her before leaving her alone and going to play the game.

Nia wasn't up for long. The eight-hundred-milligram ibuprofen she had taken knocked her out.

When she awoke two hours later, she was hungry again. Nia showered and threw on something comfortable to lounge around the house in. Then she headed to the kitchen.

"Lil Mama up. I'm going to hit you back," she heard East tell whomever he was on the phone with.

She never questioned him. She didn't have a reason to. Nia wasn't insecure, and she was comfortable and, most importantly, content with who she was and where she stood in East's life. Her position was secure, and she felt like a priority, not because she was being delusional, but because East's actions spoke louder than his words.

East talked a lot of good shit, but he also backed it up with his actions. When he told her they were going to do something or go somewhere, that was what happened. When he told her he would call her back in an hour or would bring her lunch, he did it. It was important for Nia to be with someone who stuck to their word. She desired a stable and a reliable man, and East was both of those.

His words told her that he cared for her, but his actions showed her that he truly loved her. He looked at her like she was a queen, but then he also treated her like she was royalty. East showered her with gifts, beautiful diamonds, trips, and shopping sprees, and then he showered her with love, time, and attention. They had learned each other—what turned them on and off; what their likes and dislikes were, their goals and aspirations; what their pasts had been and what they wanted their future to be—and they had grown from there.

Together, they were building a lasting relationship on a solid foundation.

"Tell bae I said hey," Nia teased as she passed by him and went into the kitchen, in hopes of finding something to eat.

"Fuck outta here," he said back.

Nia thought it was funny when she joked around about him talking to other bitches, but East did not find it funny at all. He prided himself on being committed to Nia and wanted her to take him seriously, because he was taking their relationship seriously and putting his all into it.

"What do you have a taste for?" she asked after she had walked into the living room.

East paused the game and looked at his lady. "You know I'll eat anything right now. I'm high as hell," he said.

Nia suggested ordering delivery. "What about pizza or Chinese?"

He shook his head. "Nah. I was thinking cheesesteaks," he told her.

"Babe, we gotta go get those," she whined.

East hopped up from the couch. "Call the order in, and I'll go pick them up." His mind was now set on a juicy cheesesteak with extra cheese and onions.

"I want to go with you." She came closer to him and lazily wrapped her arms around his waist and leaned her head against his chest. He laughed and hugged her back.

"I'm coming right back," he promised.

"I want to go," she said again.

East didn't protest. He knew that she was being emotional and clingy because she was on her menstrual cycle. Normally, Nia's lazy ass would stay home and work or read until he returned with food.

They both threw on sneakers and left the house. East stopped at the gas station and grabbed a two-liter bottle of Sprite and some more blunts. He planned on pouring up the syrup and kicking back with his girl tonight.

"I'll stay in the car," Nia told him when they pulled up to the Hoagie Shack.

"Yeah, with that on, I wasn't letting you get out, anyway," he said and laughed.

East discreetly tried to put his gun in his jeans, but she saw him doing it, and they exchanged eye contact.

"Safe, never sorry." He kissed her cheek and got out of the car.

She never took her eyes off him. Nia would die if something were to happen to her man, and if he felt as if he couldn't even walk without a gun into the Hoagie Shack in the hood where he grew up to grab something to eat, then something must be brewing.

East didn't disclose his street affairs or issues with her, and technically, she never asked.

Once they were back home and were sitting together at the kitchen table, eating their greasy cheesesteaks, East noticed that Nia was very quiet. She usually wasn't a chatterbox, but she hadn't mumbled two words since they made it back to the house.

"You don't like your food, baby?" he asked. His greedy ass had already scarfed down one cheesesteak, and he was now on his second one.

She laid her greasy, overloaded cheesesteak on the paper plate and took a deep breath. "What do you do?" she asked.

East had known this shit was coming sooner or later. Things had been going entirely too smoothly between the two of them since they rekindled their flame.

"I hustle."

He wasn't disclosing too much if she didn't ask for it. Nia waited on him to continue, but he didn't.

"East, I'm being serious right now." She crossed her arms and sat back in her chair.

"Babe, what you wanna know? I'm a street nigga," he told her, with a mouth full of chewed-up food.

She turned her head in order not to gag at the sight of all that mashed-up food in his mouth.

"I want to know exactly what you do. Are we safe here? Will someone come in here and tie my ass up? Don't forget I've been down this road before," she snapped.

East didn't want to have this conversation right now, or tonight or tomorrow. He hated that Nia compared him to Biggs. Although she had never come out and made it obvious, he knew she did it.

Biggs had been a made nigga, a certified hustler, and he had been the king around these parts for quite some time. East wasn't trying to replace the memories she had made with him, nor was he in competition with a nigga who had died years ago. He was his own person, and Nia needed to remember that.

He made sure their eyes had met before he spoke, because he meant the words that came from his mouth. "I would die before I let something happen to you."

East loved Nia with everything in him, and even if he rarely said it, he knew for a fact that his actions expressed his love for her. Not only was he, at this very moment, sacrificing a weekend, during which he could easily rake in a few grand, but he was also in the house with her, playing nurse, with pride.

When Nia needed something, he made sure his li'l mama had it. There were days when he was so high and stressed and wanted to be alone so he could clear his head, but she would call and say her day was stressful too and she needed to be around him, and he would come. In a heartbeat, East was by her side.

"I know that," she admitted.

She felt his protection around her, even when they weren't together. She had wanted to ask him for quite some time if he'd hired security guards to protect her, but it was obvious that he had.

"So, don't question me about how I get my money," he retorted, his tone firm.

He had to speak in a firm tone to her so she would take him seriously. East and Nia joked and played around so much that she must have forgotten who the fuck he was.

His business dealings and *that* part of his life weren't Nia's concern. There were no drugs or dirty guns at his home, and as long as she was in his bed, there wouldn't be shit popping at his crib. Even prior to meeting Nia, East hadn't shit where he slept. His house was his home, his safe haven, and with Nia being there as often as he was, he had beefed up the alarms and security at his crib.

"I love you. I'm sorry," she said, apologizing, not wanting to upset him.

He didn't say anything. Instead, he picked up his cheesesteak and finished eating, so Nia did the same. After they discarded their trash, East threw the kitchen trash bag into the larger trash can on the street, not wanting his house to smell like onions and bell peppers.

Nia was in the bathroom, brushing her teeth and washing her hands, when her man entered the bathroom to do the same.

After she spit a mouthful of mouthwash into the sink, she asked him, "Are you mad at me?"

He shook his head. "Mad for what? I know you be worried about me. I like that shit." He winked his eye.

East wasn't an argumentative person, and he was the reason why their relationship was so carefree. Nia had tried on several occasions to come at him with some bullshit, but he would shut her down mid-sentence or tell her to have a good day and hang the phone up. He had enough shit going on in the streets and wouldn't allow the one good and constant thing in his life to piss him off.

Nia wiped her mouth with the hand towel and touched his back before she left the bathroom and climbed into bed.

East asked her, "You gon' stay up for me?" He was about to drink and smoke and enjoy the rest of his night.

She tried to stifle a yawn. "Yep, boo," she told him.

Hours later, Nia was about to doze off, so she texted her boyfriend and told him good night. It wasn't a minute later that East was walking through the door.

"Nah, you can't go to sleep yet, baby," he told her in a husky tone.

Nia rubbed her eyes and sank down farther into the Sleep Number mattress. "Huh?" She was confused.

"I'm horny," he said, his words slurred.

She reminded him that she was on her cycle, and he would have to wait a few days before they could resume sexual activity. East wasn't trying to make love to her right now. He had seen enough blood throughout his day, fucking around with these trifling niggas.

"Come here. I got something for you," he whispered, pulling his shorts and boxers down and letting them drop to his ankles.

Nia whined, "Babe." She was far from horny right now. In fact, sleep was on her mind, not sex.

"Do it for a li'l bit?" he asked.

Nia rolled over and brought her lips down toward the tip of his dick and planted one big, juicy kiss on the head. "Muh." She made sure a drop of saliva rolled down to the base of his penis.

"Nah, nah. Suck it, okay?" East asked her.

She moved around to get comfortable and discovered that because East was so tall, his dick and her lips were at the correct angle.

"Shit," he whispered after Nia wet his dick up using her lips.

She did not expect to be so turned on by giving her man head, especially since she was not getting anything out of it. East's moans and grunts encouraged her to go harder, and before she knew it, she was begging him to fuck her mouth and cum down her throat.

"Damn, baby," he moaned loudly.

Nia was sucking his balls and stroking his dick at the same damn time. He couldn't watch her anymore. Her sexy lips were too much for him to admire right now.

East was focused on how good the sloppy toppy was, and if he had to judge his baby girl, he'd say this was the best head she had given him thus far.

Nia wouldn't let up on sucking and swallowing his balls. Whenever he got comfortable with her doing one motion, she would switch up and do another.

"Fuck, fuck, fuck," East grunted as his release raced through his penis, then squirted from the tip of his dick down Nia's throat. The overflow caused her lips to be coated in his cream.

She took it a step further and used East's still rock-hard dick to smear it all over her lips. "Aah," she said hungrily, wanting all of it in her mouth.

East's eyes damn near bulged out of their sockets. His li'l mama was acting like a porn star right now.

"Thanks, boo. I needed that," East told her after he'd washed up and joined her in bed.

The couple lay together in the dark, spooning and basking in what had just taken place. Nia didn't know what had come over her, but she was looking forward to doing it again. Pleasing her man felt so damn good.

"Anything for you, my love," she told him, and she meant every word.

There wasn't anything she wouldn't do for East, because in her heart she trusted he would do the same.

East kissed her neck and whispered in her ear, "I feel the same way, lady."

She blushed and smiled, even though he couldn't see her. She was sure the room was full of good vibes and sweet love, because that was what they both gave off whenever they were in each other's company.

"Love you," she whispered before closing her eyes and falling asleep.

"What's wrong with these?" Nia asked East.

The couple was out doing what they did best, shopping.

It was rare that Nia took a Monday off from work. She preached to entrepreneurs and aspiring business own-ers that Sunday and Monday were the two most import-ant days of the week. Sunday afternoons should be spent with family, relaxing and rejuvenating in order to conquer the challenges of the upcoming week. On Sunday night, a business owner should be in bed by 10:00 p.m. to ensure that he or she got an adequate amount of rest. A successful and productive Monday morning was the foundation to a great week. Sending and responding to e-mails, making follow-up calls, scheduling meetings, and going over a to-do list for the week should be at the top of the agenda and should be completed before the start of business on Monday.

However, when Nia arose on this particular Monday morning, the only thing on her mind was shoes and denim. After taking a walk in the park behind East's home, she showered and made breakfast, then went to jump on a very tired East.

He rolled over and complained of having got only two hours of sleep before Nia came in and woke him up. She argued back that no one had told him to stay out all night, doing nothing. When East mumbled under the pillow that he had been kicking it with Harlem, she had to bite her tongue and keep her thoughts to herself. The only reason Nia had yet to say anything to East about Harlem's attitude toward her was that the two did business together, and she didn't want to come in between them. However, the next time Harlem came to her on some disrespectful shit, she would not hesitate to tell East.

Nia decided to give her man a few more hours of sleep, so she spent the earlier part of the morning moving her schedule around so she could spend the rest of the day with her man, whenever he decided to rise from the dead and show her some attention.

After mind-blowing, toe-curling, "screaming from the top of their lungs" sex and another shower, East and Nia were out the door and headed to Manhattan to fuck some commas up, and it would be East's treat, of course.

The couple stopped at the Giuseppe Zanotti store first. Nia picked up a pair of men's sandals. She thought they were so fresh, but East didn't agree.

"Nothing, bae. I don't wear sandals," he told her. He was busy looking at a pair of all-black sneakers with silver soles.

She frowned. "You wear sandals around the house," she reminded him.

He didn't understand what the big deal was about him not finding the sandals appealing. "Nia, what's the issue?" he asked.

She shrugged her shoulders. "Nothing. I like the sandals. I want you to get them," she said, holding them out for him to grab.

East snickered. "I'm not spending five hundred dollars on some sandals when I have a few pair of Nike sandals at the house," he told her straight up.

He enjoyed shopping just as she did, but he wasn't designer crazy like his girl was.

"I'll get them," she said nonchalantly.

"I don't want you to get them. If I wanted them, I would have bought 'em." He didn't like how she was talking to him.

Nia shook her head and walked off.

After East checked out at the Giuseppe store, he walked across the mall to the Prada store, where Nia had found a bag she wanted.

"You see anything else you want, baby?" he asked her.

"Yes." She smiled sheepishly, not wanting to seem greedy.

The salesperson laughed at Nia and told East, "It was a lavender wallet she had her eye on."

East told the salesperson to go grab it, and then he turned his attention back to his girlfriend.

"Why are you acting crazy?" he asked.

She looked down nervously. "Do you think I'm making you spend money unnecessarily?" she asked him.

Nia knew she spent a lot of money, but it wasn't as if she was *blowing* through her funds. She had several sources of income and was nowhere near becoming broke or going bankrupt. She was a very careful spender and had several accountants and an experienced business manager to make sure she didn't jump overboard. Anytime Nia wanted to spend more than ten thousand dollars, she would have to call her accountant's office in Los Angeles, California, and have the funds wired into her account. Many people probably assumed that the few prepaid debit cards in her Gucci wallet were loaded with money, but that was far from the truth. For safety reasons, she didn't carry much cash on her, and there was not a large amount of money on the prepaid cards she used for everyday purchases.

"I'm grown, boo. You not making me do nothing I don't want to do, and besides, you earned all this shit and much more." He kissed her forehead and tugged on a belt loop on the jeans she wore.

Nia wanted more than a simple forehead kiss. She reached up on her tippy toes and puckered her lips, desiring a real kiss from her man. East bent down and planted a juicy kiss on her lips.

"I love you," he told her.

She blushed and told him that she loved him way more.

"The total is three thousand two hundred fifty dollars," the salesperson said once she had rung up the purse and the wallet.

East held his heart, as if he were having a heart attack due to the price. "Whew!" He wiped invisible sweat from his forehead.

Nia held on to his arm as he counted out the number of one-hundred-dollar bills it took to pay for her items.

"Thanks, babe," she said with excitement after the salesperson handed East the shopping bag. Nia could not wait to carry her new purse tomorrow.

"Yeah, yeah. Lunch on you," he teased.

She told him, "No pressure, Daddy," and winked her eye before walking ahead of him and into the next store.

East tossed his head back and looked up in the air, thinking, *What have I got myself into today?*

His phone rang at that moment, so he halted just inside the next store, wondering what Harlem wanted.

Nia jogged toward the front of the store, where East was standing with all their shopping bags. She saw that her boyfriend was on the phone, so she held up the six-inch pump and pointed to it.

East nodded his head, motioning to her that she could get it.

"Do you like it?" she whispered, not wanting to interrupt his conversation.

"Yeah, babe. Why you whispering?" he asked her.

"Well, you're on the phone," she said, knowing how she was when she was handling business. Nia hated to be interrupted.

"It's just this nigga Harlem. You good. Get the shoes," he told her.

East saw the expression on Nia's face turn from happy to irritated, but before he could comment, she told him okay and walked off.

"Shit, I see you busy, boy. Get at me later." Harlem was now ready to end the conversation.

"My bad, man. Nia spoiled ass got me out shopping," he told his best friend.

East knew he was delighted that she wasn't working today. It was rare that they spent the entire day together, which was one of the reasons why he was counting down to their next vacation.

"Word. She used to do my cousin the same way," Harlem said.

East knew he was throwing shade, but unlike Nia, he didn't bite his tongue for no fucking body. "Oh, word?"

Harlem laughed coolly. "Yeah, you know how them Brooklyn chicks be. Anyways, hit my jack later," he said and then hung up the phone.

East was not feeling how Harlem had come at him, and he planned to bring it up the next time he saw him.

"You done already?" East asked Nia as she walked toward him.

She nodded her head. "Yep. I got the shoes and you something too."

"Why didn't you tell me to come pay?" he asked.

She put her shades on her face and grabbed his hand. "Baby, we ain't worried about no money," she told him straight up.

Instantly, he felt his dick growing hard. Nia was a rider and a boss, and she was all his. The comment she had just made turned him on. They weren't keeping score of who spent what, and that was another reason, out of a million, he rocked with her the way he did.

Slowly, Nia was becoming his favorite downtime. It was rare to see his face in the place these days. East had more fun kicking it with his girl than he did with niggas in the streets, including the one he had started with, Harlem.

Fuck what that nigga Harlem was talking about, he thought. He didn't care what she used to do with her ex. What mattered now was that they held each other down, and he was the only nigga digging in her guts.

Back home after a long day, Nia changed out of the tight jeans she wore and into something more comfortable to lounge around in and do laundry.

"You're about to go?" she asked East after he kissed her collarbone and she noticed he had keys in his hand.

He brushed her hair back and stared into her eyes. "Not for long, beautiful," he promised.

"You're 'not for long' is really until after midnight, East," she said, saddened that he was about to leave her home alone.

"Gotta go make everything we just spent," he teased.

Nia plopped down on the couch and flicked him a middle finger. "Blah-blah. Bring me back something to eat," she told him.

"I'll call you when I'm on the way," he said.

She hated to see him go. The streets didn't come with life insurance, and she was always worried that the day would come when he didn't return.

East walked behind the couch and toward the front door. Before he could unlock it and walk out, he heard her say, "Be safe, babe."

He was always safe, but he knew she was speaking from past experience.

"Come lock the door and turn the alarm on," he told her before closing the door behind him.

Nia watched him get into his car from the window before rising from where she sat and doing as he'd instructed.

She was aware of the situation she had allowed herself to get into when they first began to grow closer together. He was in the streets, but she still didn't know how deeply he was rooted there or the bullshit he faced on a daily.

"God, please keep your hand on him . . . ," Nia whispered, struggling to speak out, feeling overwhelmed with emotion. "I can't stand to lose another . . . another love," she sighed.

11

"I'm all in her head; she's all in my bed. I'm locked and loaded, ready to go like a gun that don't jam."

– Kevin Gates, Trey Songz,
Ty Dolla $ign, and Jamie Foxx

"I love that you got these for me," East said in between licks around Nia's dark nipples.

She bolted up from the comfortable position she was in. "Who said I got 'em for you?" she asked in reference to her newly pierced nipples.

On a whim, she had allowed Samone to get crazy with her piercing gun. She had not only gotten her nipples pierced but her clitoris as well.

It had been about two weeks since she came home and surprised Daddy with the piercings, and Nia swore with her hand on the Bible that the piercings enticed East and had turned her man into a porn star. She'd sent multiple messages to Samone, thanking her for the encouragement to proceed with the piercings. Nia had had a few tattoos that she got during her teenager days, but until two weeks ago, she hadn't had any piercings.

"I know these for me," he said cockily, pushing her back down and crawling in between her legs.

She bit her bottom lip as East placed a piece of ice in his mouth from the cup that he had been sipping on while the couple enjoyed a rented movie.

"What you about to do with that?" she asked nervously.

East ignored her and towered over her body, allowing the melting ice to drip from her collarbone down to her belly button. He wasn't sure what part of her body he wanted to fuck with first, but what he did know was that it was going down tonight.

Friday nights were now reserved for all the nuts he didn't get to bust during the week. Nia had been running around like a chicken with its head cut off. She was knee-deep in orders and had recently decided to open a flagship store in Los Angeles. East had been waiting on her to tell him that she was moving. He had heard her discussing travel arrangements over the past few weeks.

When the day came for them to discuss Los Angeles, he was prepared to tell her he was going with her. His cousin, Papa, knew people everywhere, and East could move weight wherever he was. Over his dead body would he allow his girl to be parading around L.A. without him. He was cool with her taking weekend trips when she had to attend a fashion show or speak at a college, but to be gone for more than seventy-two hours? East wasn't having it.

Sleeping without his baby girl was a struggle, and for that reason, they didn't spend too many nights apart. Nia constantly asked him if she was getting on his nerves and if he wanted a break, but he would tell her no in a heartbeat. They respected each other's space, even when they were under the same roof, and that was enough for him.

"Babe, what you about to do?" a naked and horny Nia asked her boyfriend again.

She was ready to get things on and popping. He sucked the ice before pulling it in between his teeth and lowering his head down to her honey cove.

"No!" she shrieked.

The ice was cold, but once his tongue pushed farther into her, it melted and lust turned into love. With grace and patience, East took his time stroking Nia with his tongue. Every now and then he would kiss the pussy with passion.

"East, I can't take it anymore!" Nia pleaded.

Her body had succumbed to his touch, and there wasn't a drop of cum left in her. They had been participating in a very intense session of foreplay for the past hour. If he wasn't using his tongue or his lips, then he would make use of his long, manicured fingers.

Her body needed a break, but East did not plan to give her a time-out anytime soon.

"Cum then," he mumbled in between licking her pussy, blowing on her clit, and toying with the hoop that hung from in between her lips.

Nia closed her eyes and took a deep breath. Her chest heaved up and down, and she felt her heartbeat increasing. He strapped her down using his strong arms and began to fuck her pussy using his tongue. His head bobbed in and out, causing cream to form and pour from her like a volcano.

"Yes, baby, yes!" Nia said, encouraging him as she felt herself cumming.

He cleaned her up before kissing her slowly on the inside of her thighs and lapping up the remainder of her love spill. East shook his head and chuckled as he got out from between her legs.

"You be confusing me, Ma. You tell me to stop, and then, when I speed up, like, you want me to keep going," he said as he lay on top of her.

Nia's eyes were still closed. She was coming off the orgasmic high that he had given her.

"Wake up," East told her.

East bit down on her nipple before replacing his teeth with his thumb and index finger. He was enthusiastic with her nipples and had not played with them this much in the almost seven months they had been communicating and falling in love with each other.

"You need to get my name right here," he commented, kissing the space in between her boobs.

She nodded her head. "Okay, baby."

Nia wanted sleep, but the way her man's penis was set up, all rock hard and leaning against her leg, she knew sleep wasn't in the forecast.

"Sit up and bend that ass over. You already know how I want it." East smacked her thigh.

Nia grunted and smacked her lips, but she obeyed him. She assumed the position, arching her back, resting on her elbows, and placing her ass in his view.

"No twerking for Daddy tonight? What I gotta do? Pull out the ones?" he asked, kissing her ass cheeks.

"Ones?" Nia asked, turning around and looking at him.

East laughed and pulled himself up from the floor. "Let me go get some hundreds out of the safe."

Nia was sleepy. She was prepared to fuck his brains out so she could shower and go to sleep. "It's okay, baby. I'll get it from you tomorrow," she said quickly.

East smirked. "Word?"

She nodded her head and began to play with her very sensitive clit, trying to juice her pussy back up so he could have easy access and could get his off.

East ran his dick up and down her leaking pussy.

"I'm about to fuck you so good," he whispered in her ear before he sat back up and inserted his dick in her.

Nia's pussy creamed as soon as he entered her.

"Oh, fuck yes," she exclaimed.

No matter how many times the couple partook in any sexual activity, it was always new and refreshing. As soon as she thought she had learned her man, he would surprise her with some new and freaky shit. Proudly, Nia could proclaim that her man was the best she had ever had.

Biggs still crossed her mind from time to time, but not as often as before. With his birthday approaching, she would soon visit his grave site, as she did every year, but this time she wanted East to go with her.

It was important that he understood that Biggs's role in her life was vital, and that he was a very important aspect of her life. In fact, Nia considered her time with him one of the most influential chapters in her life story.

She would never forget the trials and tribulations she had gone through with him, the situations she had found herself in. But it wasn't just the tears that she had cried that were seared on her memory. The joy and the happiness that he had brought her were unforgettable too. Biggs was Biggs. He had made her who she was.

Nia had been lost before meeting him, and he had found her soul and made her a person. Openly, she gave him that credit, because she knew at the end of the day and at the bottom of her heart, there wasn't another person whom she had allowed into her mind. Biggs had broken her guard down and then had built it back up in a weird way when he died.

After Biggs, many men had tried to date her, and some had even been courageous enough to attempt to marry her, but Nia had refused to give the pussy away or drop to her knees. It was as if men from all over the world had known that she was a rare gem, and they had all wanted to claim her as theirs, but Nia had never obliged. She hadn't been able to take any of them seriously. She'd thought no one was worth the sacrifice of calling off work or canceling meetings to go out of town. There wasn't one person that had made her feel as if they deserved her time or attention.

But then East had come into her life, and before she knew it, he had turned her the fuck out. Like Biggs would always tell her, "A real nigga knows a real bitch when he sees one."

Regardless of how Harlem or anyone from the hood felt about her dating East, she was happy, and that was all that mattered to her.

Nia was very active on social media, and often, she would post a picture under the hashtag she had created, #dinnerplatesanddates. But she didn't post pictures of East that showed his face. For instance, when they were shopping, she would capture a glimpse of him checking out at the counter, without his face showing, and she would post that. Or some nights Nia would come home to a drawn bath and takeout on glass plates, and she would take a picture and post it in black and white.

There was a big difference between being discreet and being secretive. Many women often confused the two. They didn't have a conversation about their relationship being made public, because it wasn't necessary. But Nia ran a million-dollar empire, and she didn't see the purpose of posting photos of her man that revealed his identity. East was in the streets, and he lived by the code and by a popular saying, "No face, no case."

Now, if Nia wanted to post a picture of herself and her man, she could. That was where the confusion came into play in today's society. There were a lot of women out there with off guards and screen shots, but no selfies with their "man." Discretion and secretiveness. People had to learn the difference between the two.

"Damn, baby. You don't hear me talking to you?" East said, exasperated.

East had slowed his strokes down. He got his rocks off when Nia talked shit to him, but she hadn't said anything in the past two minutes.

"Sorry, baby," she said, apologizing.

East's dick went limp as he pulled out of her.

"What's wrong?" he asked.

She shook her head. "Nothing, baby. Something came across my mind. I am sorry. I can get you right," she told him happily.

Nia was far from a selfish lover, and East had been catering to her body all night. She knew that he, too, had had a long week, so it wouldn't be cool to send him to bed with full balls when he had taken the time to drain every single ounce of cum from her body.

East didn't protest. He leaned back and stretched his legs.

"Daddy misses this tongue?" she cooed, talking directly to the tip of his penis.

"Nah, Daddy misses the back of that throat," he said coolly.

Nia smacked her lips and ignored him as she took him in her mouth and made love to her man's dick without using her hands.

"Hell yeah," East grunted, smacking her ass and sticking his thumb in her butt.

He was such a nasty man, but Nia wouldn't have it any other way. If she couldn't be a freak behind closed doors and between the sheets with the man she shared a bed with every night, then whom could she be nasty with?

As she stood in front of forty-two employees in the conference room of a building she had recently purchased and renovated, Nia was feeling nervous, hot, and clammy. Today was the launch of her new business venture, and she wanted the day to be successful.

The night before, she had drunk two cups of hot tea and had said her prayers before she lay down to sleep.

East knew how important today was, so last night he had stayed at home and she had stayed at her condo, and they had texted until she fell asleep. Now Nia was wishing that she had allowed him to come over last night, when he'd jokingly suggested that some of his dick would take the nerves off.

Oh, how badly she wanted some of her man right now.

"Nia, when do you plan on starting?" asked Nickey, the vice president of her company.

Nia nodded her head and cleared her throat before cracking her neck and spitting the gum she had been chewing on for the past hour or so into a blank piece of paper.

Her hair was beginning to curl up, and she regretted not getting a sew-in when she was at the hair salon last night. Today she wore her natural hair pressed, something she normally didn't do. The wide-legged navy blue pantsuit she wore was coupled with a crème shell and crème Jimmy Choo pumps. She had opted out of makeup, since no cameras were present for today's first meeting.

"Nia," Nickey said again.

Everyone they invited had been sitting at the round tables for almost thirty minutes, waiting on the meeting to begin.

"Give me a fucking second," Nia hissed before stepping off the stage and walking out of the room.

Kate, who was now officially Nia's assistant, left the wall that she had been leaning against and followed her out of the room. Nia paced the floor and counted to ten.

Why the fuck am I sweating so bad? she thought to herself.

Kate gave her a few seconds to pull herself together before she touched her arm and told her, "You got this. You have worked on this for four months. I have watched you day in and day out. There were some nights when I left you in the office, and when I came back the next day, you were still there. This is what you've been waiting for and working hard for."

Nia wiped a lone tear that had fallen down her face. She nodded her head, agreeing with Kate.

Like most entrepreneurs who had risen from the bottom through hard work and hadn't slept their way to the top or sold their soul, Nia was worried. She struggled with failing and battled fear. Some evil creature lurking in the back of her head had been creeping around her brain all day. It had been weakening her confidence with its negative assessments of her all day.

Who do you think you are?

You are a drug dealer's girlfriend!

You sold your body before he met you, young slut!

Your mama was a whore, and your daddy was a thief.

Have you forgotten where you come from?

You and that dark skin . . . The fashion industry does not accept you.

She was going through mental warfare, which was common with business owners. Nia knew that the paperwork was right and the contracts were correct, but she still continued to sabotage herself, never feeling like anything she did was enough or was acceptable. It was true that she was a girl from the projects, that she'd been raised in public housing, and that she hadn't had more than ten dollars to her name at any time until she met Biggs.

But so the fuck what!

She shook her head and took her confidence back. She cracked her neck and stretched her arms over her head.

After one look at Kate, who nodded her head and encouraged her to begin the meeting, Nia whispered, "I got this!"

Kate clapped her hands. "Yes, Ms. Hudson, you do!"

Nia reentered the conference room and decided to walk the floor instead of taking a seat with the rest of her advisory board.

"Good morning," she said, with a huge smile, as she scanned the room.

A few people said good morning back, but it wasn't enough of a response to satisfy Nia.

"I said, 'Good morning!'" she repeated.

The feedback was better this go-round.

"I am Nia Hudson, founder, visionary, creator, and lead designer of ND Studios, Nia Hudson Designs, and every other company I own," she said and then laughed, and everyone else did as well. Nia took a deep breath. "Will y'all judge me if I take these heels off?" she asked.

Some of the women in the room understood exactly how she felt, so they told her to take 'em off and get comfortable. Nia removed her shoes, and Kate came and snatched them up.

"Many of you have gone through several rounds of interviews, and first, I want to say congratulations! I know my team is hell to work with, but the good thing is, you made it," Nia said.

Many people agreed with her there. The process had been an extensive one.

"I've always had this theory that I can do anything I set my mind to, and in the Bible it tells us that we can do all things through Christ, who strengthens us," Nia told the room. "One night my assistant and I—if you have not met her yet, you will soon—we were leaving a fashion show, and I told her about a great idea I had, and she was like, 'Oh my God, Nia, yes! That sounds perfect. Let's do it.'"

Nia clapped her hands together and went on. "So, that's why you are all here. Some of you guys are bloggers, photographers, makeup artists, hairstylists, seamstresses, tailors, models, designers, or stylists. I have researched each and every one of you. I have stalked your social media and have called your middle school teachers. I even called some of y'all bosses. I got all in ya business, but do you know why?"

A few people raised their hand to answer the question, but Nia didn't want any responses.

"Because I worked hard to get to where I am, and for quite some time, it was just me and a few other hard-working people," Nia stated. "My team will tell you, Nia does not play that. There were just a few of us, and we had fun traveling. You know, the perks are cool, but we worked ten times harder than we played. My brand means everything to me. I came from nothing, and to have it all now not only humbles me but also keeps me grounded and focused."

She walked the room as she continued. "You have been carefully chosen to represent my brand, while creating your own at the same time. My resources are now yours. For forty percent, studios, event access, models, prints, fabrics, designs, everything is now yours," she said excitedly.

After the first team meeting with her new employees ended, they were all given personal tours of the building, were handed an ID, and were assigned to a room. The building contained six large workrooms—a concept room for the fashion designers; a sewing room for the seamstresses and tailors; a hair salon for the hairstylists; a makeup room for the makeup artists; a photography room for the photographers; and a room with a practice runway for the models. Each room was equipped with a large closet full of the supplies, everything a person would need to create and produce. There was also a smaller room for the bloggers.

The building also came equipped with a large auditorium for fashion shows. Fashion shows had to be funded by the fashion designers and all those involved themselves. Nia wasn't responsible for pushing a designer's brand or clothing line. In addition, the building had a green room and a lobby for events. To bring in extra revenue, Nia planned to make the auditorium available for aspiring and current designers to rent.

On the main floor of the building was a business center, where twelve administrators worked to help the people now employed by Nia Hudson book jobs and keep their schedules organized. The building also had a private parking garage and a public parking lot. The entire area was surveyed by cameras, and Nia had a full security team on staff. There was also a lunchroom, and Kate had arranged for restaurants in the area to drop in and sell food throughout the day.

Nia was very pleased with how everything was going so far with the new business venture, and she had a big surprise for her staff back at ND Studios, where her office would still be, along with the rest of her own design team's offices. She knew the magic she had created at her design studio, and she was as committed as ever to that endeavor.

Once a month, she would choose a designer from the new venture to sell his or her pieces in the boutique at ND Studios. The ideas and possibilities were endless with her new business venture, and she was ready to see people's dreams come true, and make some money in the process.

After finishing her orientation duties at the new building, Nia and her ND Studios team gathered for dinner at Barry's, a steak house in Lower Manhattan.

"We did it," she said happily, toasting to everyone, as she sat at the head of the table.

A few minutes later, Nia noticed that everyone was looking away from the table, so she turned around to see what had captured their attention. Standing behind her in a tailor-made suit—something she had never seen him wear—was her boyfriend, with a bouquet of white roses in his hand.

"Baby," she called out, and then she jumped out of her seat and trotted up to him. She wrapped her arms around him and gave him a big hug.

Today had been extremely long and hectic. Nia had run home after orientation ended and had showered before her makeup artist arrived to do her makeup for the press conference that preceded tonight's dinner. But the press conference had run over, and she hadn't got a chance to change into the dress she specifically ordered for tonight's dinner with her team.

East had sent her a few celebratory messages through-out the day, which she'd responded to hours after he sent them. He'd known she would be busy all day and hadn't expected a response. He'd just wanted her to know that she was on his mind and he was proud of her.

"Congratulations, baby," he whispered in her ear.

East peeped the stares and heard the whispers. Not too many people were aware that Nia Hudson had a romantic side. They all figured she probably had *some-one*, considering the giddy atmosphere around the office of late, but only Kate, her lawyer, her publicist, and her business manager had met East.

Nia inhaled East's scent. Citrus and weed tickled her nose. Her man had rid his face of the scruffy look he had been rocking for the past few months, and he had cleaned up well.

She blushed. "You look so good," she told him in his ear, making sure her tongue grazed his earlobe.

He hugged her back and told her to be a good girl.

Nia turned around, and without her asking, Nickey, the vice president of her company, moved down one chair so East could take a seat near Nia.

"We were about to have dessert. Join us," Nia told him.

East shook his head. "I'm going to have a drink at the bar. Enjoy your people, boo," he told her and handed her the roses.

"Are you sure?" Her eyes searched his face for sincerity.

He flashed her that famous bad-boy smile and told her, "Yeah, baby."

She smiled at him and then redirected her attention to the table, as if East had never stolen the show. Nia took her seat and resumed the toast, and all around the table, personalized champagne glasses clinked as Nia's comrades all said, "*Salud!*"

Everyone was delighted with the new business venture, though they knew there was a lot of hard work ahead to make it a success. As Nia would always say on Monday mornings, when she entered the office and passed all her employees, "It's grind time."

"Shit, you been on it lately, li'l cuz?" Papa said, praising his cousin. He was happy to see the li'l nigga getting on his feet.

East kept a cool look on his face, but it felt good to have his cousin pay him a compliment. In the dark and gritty streets of New York City, it wasn't too often that another man paid homage or gave credit where it was due. Papa wasn't like that, though. Plus, they were family, blood cousins at that.

Harlem stood off to the side, steaming. East wasn't moving the weight by himself, but Harlem wouldn't call him out. He didn't understand why Papa wouldn't fuck with them with a discounted price. Papa knew that they were basically getting raped in terms of prices, but he refused to do business with East.

Every time they ran into Papa in the streets, Harlem always felt like Papa belittled East, and in his opinion, East was too damn dumb to recognize the talking down.

"What you doing this weekend? You and ya shorty should slide to L.A. with Demi and me. My homeboy's wife is an artist, and she got a li'l art show and shit," Papa said to East.

East nodded his head. Nia would love to shoot out to L.A., especially since she had been tiptoeing around the house while on the phone with her team, discussing a boutique there.

"I'm going to run it by her and see what she says," he told his cousin.

Papa dapped him up and then said to Harlem, "You quiet today, ain't ya?"

Papa noticed everything about Harlem, and today wasn't the first time he had picked up on negative vibes.

Papa could never get East by himself long enough to sit him down. Every time he reached out, Harlem was either riding with him or East was headed to meet up with him. Papa kept telling his cousin to stop being joined at the hip with a nigga. He preached constantly, "The only person who should know your every move is the bitch you love."

East would brush his comments off, knowing that Papa lived a very paranoid life because he was deep in the streets. His big cousin was one of the founding fathers of the Underworld. Papa was responsible for serving not just the city or the state, not even just the surrounding states. He was global.

The popular song lyric "Really I'm the plug" applied to Papa, because he *really* was the plug. There wasn't anything that the man couldn't get his hands on. His reach was expansive, and any time East found himself in a bind, his cousin was there to pull him out of it, no questions asked.

East had fucked up along the way, but when he'd come to Papa with Harlem in tow one day, East had promised him that he was ready to see some real money and wouldn't do anything to mess that up. East was from Brooklyn, but he had always fucked around in Harlem, and Papa had always told him to pick a side. Papa had looked into his cousin's eyes that day and had said that if heat came his way or toward the Underworld, he would kill him. Then he would show up at East's funeral and hold East's grandmother's and aunt's hands and act as if he had no idea what had happened.

Until Papa felt in his heart that East was really ready to get his hands dirty, he would not put him on. He showed him love every time he saw him and dropped a jewel of wisdom in his lap as well. East had been around for quite some time, but there were a few dots he hadn't yet connected together, and there was nothing that Papa could do for him. Hustling was free. It was the grind that cost you.

Harlem flashed Papa a smirk now. It was obvious they didn't really care for each other, but out of respect for East, Harlem kept things kosher. However, Papa was one of the rudest people that a person could ever come in contact with: he simply did not give a fuck what came out of his mouth.

"Nah, baby. You know it's all love," Harlem said slyly.

Papa scratched the side of his beard before turning around and speaking with his partner, who was with him on his bike as well. Papa was a motorcycle fanatic. "I don't like that nigga," he said.

East laughed off his comment. "All right, cuz. I'm about to slide. It was good seeing you, though."

He dapped and hugged Papa and prepared to head to his next destination. It wasn't too often that Papa's uncle cut East's hair, but today his barber hadn't been able to line him up, so he and Harlem had stopped by Papa's uncle's shop for a quick second, and that was how they'd run into Papa.

"Be safe, li'l bro. Let me know if Cali is in the weekend plans for y'all," Papa reminded him.

Now that East was seeing some money and, according to their gossiping family members, his girl had major cake as well, it was time for East to go play with the big dogs.

In his motorcycle's rearview mirror, Papa caught Harlem staring at him. He waved at him and then patted his gun. He did not fuck with Harlem at all. Any nigga that did the trifling and sheisty shit that Harlem had done in the past was not to be trusted.

Harlem and Papa used to run in the same circle, but Harlem had exposed his hand, and Papa hadn't liked what he saw. Ever since then, he'd kept his distance.

Imagine how pissed Papa had been when Harlem and East linked up during a stint in county jail. Harlem had secrets, and Papa could not wait until all that shit came to the light. But as long as his cousin was good, then so was Papa.

And if Harlem came for Papa's cousin on some fuck shit, that was when Papa would let his gun do the talking. If there was one the thing the Underworld had taught him over the years, it was to keep your enemies as close as you did the ones you loved. After all, they were often the first to forsake you.

12

"Straight up out the gutter . . . Now we got
90210 on our address."

– Future and Drake

"I like her for you," Demi told East as she danced to the tunes that the DJ was playing.

She was tipsy and full of life. There was something about being in Los Angeles without her children that had made her come alive. Demi had always been a good sport. A smile was forever on her face, and her warm and bubbly personality was contagious.

She and Papa were the complete opposite. He was thugged out from the crown of his head to the soles of his feet. Papa's body, like his cousin's, was covered in ink, even his eyelids and the inside of his mouth, where he had had Demi's name inked in cursive. Papa was rugged, ignorant, and obnoxious, but in the presence of his wife, he was the perfect gentleman. Together, they were the epitome of a beautiful, loving black couple.

"She the one, cuz," a drunk East told his cousin's wife.

Nia was the one. She was *it*. There wasn't another woman whom he could see himself with at this point. His grandmother had told him the other day that everything he'd gone through as a young boy—and even the other

women he'd been with, the few that he had taken seriously—prepared for him this moment. Love. Falling in
love with Nia was easy. She was everything that he had
never thought he wanted in a woman, and everything
that he now needed to survive. Her love was inspiring. It
challenged him to be a better man for her.

"What are you thinking about?" Nia asked him once
she returned from the bathroom.

He pulled her close to him and wrapped his arms
around her waist and planted a soft kiss on her forehead.
"Fucking you on the balcony when I get home," he admitted.

Nia felt her pussy jump against the satin fabric of the
nude thong she wore for tonight's festivities.

When East had proposed flying to Los Angeles with
his cousin and his wife, she'd been ecstatic. Not only did
she need to scope the town out, but Nia was also in desperate need of a getaway. She had been working tirelessly since the launch of her latest business venture.

Last night, the couples had gone to dinner and then
to a late movie. Because of jet lag, everyone had retired
early in the house they were renting for the weekend.
This morning, after brunch, East and Papa had gone to
ride dirt bikes out in the valley with Malachi, Papa's best
friend, while Demi and Nia had gone shopping.

During their shopping spree, the women had got to
pick each other's brains, and so far, Nia thought that
Demi was the coolest. It wasn't too often that Nia opened
up to anyone, not even to her own two best friends, but
Demi was so sincere and genuine that before Nia knew
it, she was dabbing the corners of her eyes in the department store as she spoke openly about how East had come
into her life and had changed her for the better. Demi

rubbed her back and told her that she knew exactly how she felt, as Papa had been her knight in shining armor.

Now the two couples were standing in a private booth in the VIP section of a popular nightclub in downtown L.A.

Nia stood next to her man's tall frame. The blush-colored, fitted, knee-length dress by Givenchy she wore fit her body perfectly. A pair of hot pink stilettos accompanied the dress, and Nia's freshly made-up face that had been painted by one of the best makeup artists in L.A. Nia had shared with her that she would be moving to the city soon and would need her for business and personal purposes. The makeup artist was elated to hear that she would have Nia Hudson as a client.

Nia's hair was pulled into a ponytail at the nape of her neck. The hairstyle was slowly becoming her signature. She gave the credit to East when people asked her what had made her start wearing her hair pushed back from her face. Over the years, she had become known for wearing bangs and a bob, or long extensions, with a few tresses covering her face, so the new look had not gone unnoticed.

Her confidence bolstered, Nia was no longer hiding behind designer frames or pulling a baseball cap down on her head when she was out in public. She was beautiful, and it had been about time she realized it. No, she wasn't in perfect shape. On some days, she was on a diet, and at other times she had a taste for two chili cheese dogs topped with onions and mustard. Imperfect? Yes, that was true. And Nia had finally learned to embrace it. No longer was she allowing the "standards" that the fashion industry had created to dictate how she lived and operated. Her brown skin was to be loved, and the first one who had to love it was her.

East had knocked down the wall that she built up, and ever since then, Nia had discovered a new kind of *sexy*. Her setbacks, her past, and even her flaws were what made her Nia Hudson.

"Damn, you smell good," Nia told East.

He was so high and drunk, he didn't even hear her, but she didn't care. They had all night to talk . . . and do other things. So that the smoke from the blunt that he was smoking would not irritate her, she turned around and leaned against his body, enjoying the good vibes in the club.

East had a bottle in one hand and the blunt in the other, but then he passed the blunt to Papa, who then passed it to Demi. Demi rarely smoked, and the few times she had, she had always been in the presence of her husband. Papa didn't play that shit.

Nia didn't smoke at all. It simply was not her thing. Nor did she knock anyone who did. She was a public figure, and she was pretty sure pictures were being taken of her right now, especially considering the way she was cozied up with her man. East and Nia didn't really do public displays of affection. The most they did together was shop and go to get food, but Nia did not give a fuck anymore. She loved her man and did not care who knew.

However, East was in the streets, and she had no clue how she would answer questions if she was asked what his profession was. Because he was so tall, people might assume that he was a D-list basketball player or that he played overseas.

As Nia enjoyed the club's good vibes, her mind wandered to her and East's future. East was such a hood nigga that his bank accounts, his insurance, and the few things he did own were not even in his name. If they were going to be together, then it was time for Nia to get her man together, starting with his finances. Nia planned to talk to him about investing some of his funds in stocks and even starting a business. And she wanted him to invest in residential properties. She had her real estate license, and she thought it would be beneficial if together, they purchased some prime real estate.

While she was deep in thought, East suddenly groped her ass and ran his hand down her spine. Nia jumped at his touch, but then she warmed up to him, backed up closer to him, and danced on his dick.

Demi called out, "Okay, girl. I see you."

Nia turned around and winked at her. They had exchanged tips on sexual techniques and how to keep things spicy in the bedroom. Demi had given her a few tips and tricks that Nia was looking forward to trying on her man.

See, Demi was a prima ballerina, so naturally, she was flexible and knew how to her work all her limbs in her man's favor. Nia's ass barely lifted her leg to grant East better access so that he could dig her guts out, but she did want to do something special for her man really soon, because he deserved it.

Before the action in the club wound down, Papa suggested they leave now in order to avoid the commotion and the traffic at closing time, and everyone agreed. Nia and East got an Uber and headed back to the house they two couples had rented. Demi and Papa were planning to stop by the store in one of Malachi's cars, which he had given Papa for the weekend, so that was why the couples were in separate vehicles.

In the back of the Uber, Nia could not keep her hands off her man. She wasn't even drunk, and she didn't want to blame raging hormones. She just found something so intoxicating about East. Nia could never get enough of the taste of his skin. Even after biting on his ears, tugging at his bottom lip, and licking and sucking his neck in the Uber, she wanted more.

She began to pull on his pants, but he told her to stop. "You ain't even trying to do that, Ma, so don't start," he warned.

She whined and went back to kissing his neck. Nia ignored her safety and took the seat belt off and plopped herself in his lap.

"I love you so much," she told him, with lust and love pouring from her eyes.

East ran his hands down the sides of her body. "I know," he said cockily.

If someone had told him that rude Nia Hudson, the woman who had brushed him off at the club that night almost a year ago, would be making out with him in the back of an Uber, he wouldn't have believed him or her.

Like a moth to a flame, they were attracted to each other, and they were damn near attached at the hip, but in a good way. Everything about him turned her on, from the way he slept and snored to the way he turned in his sleep when the air was off.

Earlier tonight, she had sat on the bed in only her bra and panties and had watched him conduct business via his trap phone and get dressed at the same time, all while smoking a blunt. Her mouth had watered then, but she'd known they had somewhere to be.

Now the night had ended, and they had all the time in the world to make love to each other. Nia was impatiently waiting on the car to arrive at their destination and come to a complete stop.

"Damn, Ma. This pussy wet," East whispered in her ear, not wanting the Indian man who was driving them back to the house to hear him praising his girl.

As he toyed with her clit beneath her dress, she moaned in his ear, "Wet for Daddy."

East leaned his head back. Nia was fucking with him tonight, and he couldn't even take it. His dick was hard as Chinese arithmetic, and at any moment, he knew it was bound to bust through the seams of his designer jeans.

"What you want me to do to you when we get home?" he asked, loving to hear Nia talk nasty to him.

She giggled before dropping her head near his ear and using her tongue excessively as she filled his head with fantasies.

The next morning, the couple lay together naked under the covers. East was still sleeping. Nia had been up for hours, working on her Mac laptop. She had set an alarm to climb back into bed before her man woke up, and he had yet to arise.

Nia huffed and puffed before removing herself from bed yet again, and then she went downstairs to the kitchen to fix a cup of coffee. The two-story, three-bedroom house overlooked the mountains and was beautiful. Papa had found the fully furnished and stocked home on the Airbnb Web site, and Nia planned on using Airbnb when she traveled for an extended stay and didn't want to be bothered with a hotel.

"Morning," Demi said cheerfully. Her tight coils were all over her head, and the petite woman was standing over the stove, flipping a pancake.

"Hi." Nia returned her greeting with just as much joy.

Nia, too, was in a great mood. Last night had been freaking amazing, and her body was now fighting against her. Not only was her back tight, but so were her legs, her arms, and even her jaw. Literally, Nia had sucked East until he fell asleep.

"I take it you had a good time last night," Demi observed and giggled.

"Yes, we did. What's on the agenda for today?" Nia replied as she poured a cup of coffee from the coffeepot. Demi must have read her mind and just brewed it.

Demi slid the pancake onto a platter and poured a small amount of the batter into the hot skillet. "Jade's art show is tonight. I'm not sure if we are doing dinner before or after. But other than that, nothing is planned. Me and Papa are going to do some shopping for the kids whenever he wakes up," she said.

Nia figured she and East would do the same, but not for children *yet*.

"How are you balancing your career, kids, and a husband?" Nia asked, desperately wanting to know how Demi, saddled with all those responsibilities, kept a smile on her face and did not pull her hair out.

Demi turned down the burner and faced Nia. "Balance, girl. Papa and I are on a very strict schedule, but technically, he's like having another child." She laughed and turned back around to tend the skillet.

"Oh really?" said a male voice.

Nia saw that it was Papa. She smiled and told him good morning as she hopped on a bar stool at the island after setting her coffee cup on the granite.

"Baby, I didn't know you were up," Demi said sarcastically.

He ignored her, went over to the stove, kissed her forehead, and snatched a piece of bacon and gobbled it down.

East was handsome, and though Nia would never look at his cousin in that way, she recognized that the man was fine as hell too. It was safe to say good genes ran in their family.

"Yeah, I'm your son, all right. You weren't saying that last night," he teased and smacked Demi on the butt.

Love was oozing from their pores, and it made Nia want to go hug on her beau.

"Don't even start," Demi giggled and kissed her husband.

"Let me go get East up," Nia said and hopped off the bar stool a little too quickly, forgetting how sore she was.

Papa saw the discomfort written on her face.

"Damn. Cuz got you like that?" He chuckled.

Demi swatted his arm and told him to mind his own business.

East was still knocked the hell out, but after a few kisses planted on him by his girlfriend, he slowly peeled his eyes open.

"What a sight to wake up to," he whispered and yawned.

That morning-after breath was horrid. Nia moved out of his way and covered her nose. "Ooh, baby," she said.

East laughed and stretched his legs. "That's your ass that got my breath stinking, literally," he teased.

She rolled her eyes and smiled a little, thinking of how crazy things had got last night.

"Demi is making breakfast. You're the only one still in bed," she informed East.

He was on vacation and wasn't ready to get out of bed. "Bring our plates in here," he suggested.

"That's rude," Nia told him and shook her head.

"Man, they don't give a fuck if we eat with them or not," he told her straight up.

Nia huffed, but she did as he'd said, and as it turned out, when she walked into the kitchen, Demi and Papa were nowhere to be found.

As she made one big plate for her and East to share, she heard a loud, piercing scream, which was followed by a "Yes, Daddy!"

"They in there doing it," Nia told East after she placed the plate and silverware beside him in the bed and went back to close and lock the door.

East laughed. "That's how you about to be in a few minutes. I need to eat and get my energy back up."

She groaned at the thought of her pussy being opened back up. She was unsure if she could go another round.

"What's wrong?" he asked.

Nia admitted that she was sore.

"Damn, boo. I'm sorry," he said, apologizing sincerely.

"No, it's okay, babe. I'm fine."

Nia had enjoyed last night too much for East to feel as if he needed to apologize. East reached over and kissed the side of her face. Nia still smelled his stinky breath.

"Babe, please go brush your teeth," she fussed as she climbed on the bed.

He erupted into laughter, then blew his hot breath in her face.

"Aahhh!" She rolled over and off the bed before mumbling, "Kill me now."

After breakfast, Nia finally talked East out of being a couch potato the entire day, and before long, they were out of the house and getting into an Uber, headed to Rodeo Drive. Their first stop was the MCM store.

"You don't need anything else," East told her as she pulled him into the MCM store.

"Babe, don't be silly. A woman's closet is never full," she said before being greeted by one of the salespersons.

"Ms. Hudson, what a pleasure to have you in the store today. Do we need to shut down, or are you comfortable with other patrons?" the woman said.

Nia told her, "They're fine. We're just browsing."

She hated when people reminded her she was a celebrity. Today she wanted to be normal and enjoy sunny California with the love of her life.

"Great! How about some champagne?" the salesperson suggested.

Nia turned and asked East if he wanted a drink. He nodded his head, and Nia asked for two glasses of champagne.

They had come into the store only to see if they had any new book bags. Nia had a few meetings out of town in the next few weeks, and she wanted to get a new book bag, something that she could haul all her things in as she went from plane to plane.

"I like this one," East told her, holding up a black monogrammed book bag.

She liked it too.

"Can we get two of these?" she asked the salesperson, who had stayed nearby to make sure that Nia was accommodated.

"Certainly, miss. Anything else in the store that sparks your interest?"

Nia looked around. "No. That's all we came for today," she told the woman, with a warm smile, and then followed her to the counter.

East went to pay for the book bags, but she hated to see him pull out such a large wad of money in front of people.

"I got it, boo," she told him quickly, and then she handed the salesperson a silver American Express business debit card.

He knew how Nia was, so there was no point in him saying anything. He smacked her on the ass and grabbed their bags when the transaction was completed.

Nia had got used to East's aggressive behavior, so she was not bothered anymore when he touched her. Without any forewarning, he would pull her hair gently and bite her neck, smack her on the ass, kiss her and then lick her lips . . . all kinds of sensual things that she now loved.

Papa and Demi flew back to New York right after the art show, but Nia and East weren't in a rush to return home. They were enjoying the city.

That night they went out for dinner.

"This is so good. Taste it."

Nia reached over the table with her fork, which held a succulent piece of a colossal shrimp dipped in yum yum sauce. East bit down on the fork, pulled the shrimp off with his tongue, and chewed.

"Damn, that is good," he agreed.

"Yep. Now let me taste yours," Nia said and then stuck her fork in his plate.

She had been eying his rib-eye steak, roasted cauliflower, and garlic potatoes since the server had brought their food to the table.

"Greedy, you getting thick too," East said, commenting on his girl's appearance.

Normally, she would have freaked out and pushed her plate away and drunk water for the remainder of the night, but because she had recently entered this new realm called "Fuck what people think," she let his comment roll off her back.

"But you like it," she shot back, knowing that he was playing.

He nodded his head and took a sip of his drink. "Love it, all of it." He eyed her.

Every now and then, Nia would change right before his eyes and become withdrawn, beset by her old worries. He didn't want to stir up her old concerns about her looks, so he made sure to compliment her now. He wanted to make sure that tonight remained perfect and ended on a great note.

"I know," she told him with pride.

Love gleamed in her eyes. Nia was content, and it truly had been a long time coming.

"My cousin has been trying to get in touch with me," she blurted out as they prepared for bed later that night.

East waited a few minutes before he responded. "Is that why you asked if we could stay a few extra days?" he asked.

She looked up at him. "Well, you didn't seem like you were rushing back, either."

He pulled her down on the bed. "Slow your roll, Li'l Mama. I'm asking, that's all," he said, comforting her.

Nia sighed. "Yes," she admitted to East.

"Are y'all not cool?"

Nia didn't bring up her family, and he had never asked before.

"No. I haven't spoken to her in years, and I don't plan on it." Her mind was made up. Those people meant her no good.

"So, what you gon' do? What if it's an emergency?" He was trying to get her to see the situation from a different angle. East knew how stubborn Nia was, but in his eyes, family was family.

"She's trifling, baby. She e-mailed me a few months ago, threatening to tell my business to a tabloid. I'm, like, 'Do it. What have I done that was so bad where people will pay you? I'm not even that famous,'" she said in an irritated tone.

"Yes, you are. You don't see it, but you are famous, babe. Today on Rodeo people were calling your name, taking pictures, and all that shit," he told her.

Nia didn't care about any of that.

"I don't want to talk to her," she whined.

East pulled her up closer to him so he could look into her eyes. She now lay atop his chest.

"Then don't, but at the end of the day, they really all the family you got," he reminded her.

She closed her eyes, then opened them again and stared at East. "But I have you," she said in a childlike tone.

"Yeah, and I ain't going nowhere."

They reached toward one another and shared a much-needed passionate kiss, and that sealed East's promise in his mind.

"I got you, boo," East reassured her.

He rubbed her back until she fell asleep. After rolling Nia over onto her side of the bed, East went into the living room to spark up a blunt. He thumbed through the few missed calls and text messages he had and decided that no one was important enough for him to return the call, including his best friend, Harlem.

When he, Papa, and Malachi went joyriding through the valley on dirt bikes, East had been presented with the proposition that he get a piece of the pie. East couldn't believe his cousin had brought this up.

East had gone to him on several occasions, asking to be put on, but every time, Papa had told him no. After careful consideration, Papa now believed that with the proper guidance, East could be well on his way to profiting in the streets.

Papa was a hot boy, and so was East. Papa was looking forward to having someone like himself to do all his dirty deeds with, as the other men in the Underworld were polished. Papa was rough around the edges and had no plans on changing who he was.

Papa prided himself on being a real hood nigga and would gladly tell the Underworld to kiss his ass whenever they warned him to chill. Until any of them stepped up to the plate to handle the grimy shit, they had nothing to say to him.

East had a lot to think about and process.

He knew without a doubt that Harlem was going to feel some type of way, but he had to think about his future. Nia was sitting on stacked bread, and East wasn't hurting for any cash, but he wanted more.

If his girl came to him asking for a five-million-dollar investment, without hesitation, East wanted to be able to support her. Right now, he wasn't in a position to do that, and Papa had told him that five million could easily be obtained.

The benefits of joining the Underworld were endless, and to be invited in, even if he wouldn't have a spot at the roundtable . . . he still considered it a blessing.

Hours later, Nia wandered into the living room after waking up to use the bathroom. Not feeling her man in the bed with her, she had gone searching for her love.

"Can't sleep?" she asked as she sauntered into the living room.

East blew a cloud of smoke out of his nose. "Got some shit on my mind, bae," he told her.

She nestled against him and kissed his neck. "Talk to me," she said, wanting to be his listening ear, just as he had been hers a few hours prior.

"Nothing for you to worry about," he said, not wanting to disclose any information until the deal was secured.

Papa had told East to give him a call when he returned home, and then they would go from there.

"Are you happy?" she asked.

East glanced down at her. "Hell yeah, baby," he told her, meaning every word.

His life hadn't been running this smoothly in quite some time. The bullshit in the streets was at a minimum. East had fewer headaches, but that was probably because he was now fucking with only one woman. Juggling all those hoes had had his mind messed up for a while. It was so much easier to be committed. Lying and dodging females was stressful, and he couldn't believe he had lived that life for so long.

"I'm happy too," Nia said.

Just like it was for East, this had been the best year of her life. Everything was going perfectly. Her businesses were thriving, her brand was worth well over a million dollars, and she was being booked left and right for speaking engagements.

Being successful and seeing her dreams become realities were not the only things that had ignited her happiness. The people around her were happy as well, and that fostered Nia's sense of well-being and contentment. Nasi would be getting married any day now. Samone's business had skyrocketed, and she was in meetings to land a reality show that would be filmed in her tattoo shop.

East was happy, and together, he and Nia were working to keep their relationship solid. Consistency and communication were the two most important elements of a lasting relationship. Remaining consistent, doing what they did to capture each other's attention and hearts, was vital. Constant communication, whether it was a good morning message or a check-in throughout the day, went a long day. People wanted to be thought of, whether they came out and admitted it or not.

So overall, Nia was one elated woman.

"Well, I have something to tell you," she announced, starting the conversation that she had been dreading for quite some time.

East removed his arm from her waist and rested one of his arms behind his head as he stretched his long legs across the ottoman. He continued to smoke as he waited on Nia to speak.

"I'm listening," he said.

She cleared her throat and sat up, wanting to face him. Nia needed to see every single facial expression he made when she revealed her news, not knowing whether he would consider it good or bad.

"So, you know business has been booming lately. I am talking about numbers have been great. I have about four wedding consultations next week," she said, rambling.

East took a deep breath. Nia was bullshitting, and he knew it. "I know, babe, and I'm proud of you," he told her, nodding his head.

She clasped her hands together and continued. "And so . . . it's time for me to expand my empire."

East smiled. "Man, come on and tell me," he said, encouraging her to continue.

"Okay, okay." She jumped up and wandered around the room, silent. He already knew what she was about to say, but he enjoyed seeing her clam up. "I have to move to California to open and oversee my new boutique, until I trust they can run it without me," she said finally, with her hands over her eyes.

Nia was so scared of what his reaction would be. She trusted that their relationship could withstand the distance. They both could travel back and forth during the week, since they both were self-employed and could make their own schedules, one of the perks of working for yourself. There were no limitations on what they could do.

"When?" East asked.

Nia sighed. "You're mad." She pouted. She'd known that he would trip.

He pulled on the blunt and drew the smoke into his lungs. "Nah, babe. I just asked how soon we're moving."

"East, I really need this right now!" she protested. "My boutique in New York . . . Wait, what did you say?" She knew she hadn't heard him correctly, or *had* she?

He smiled at his beautiful girlfriend as she plopped into his lap.

"Did you say *we*?" she asked, kissing him all over his face.

East laughed and held one of her ass cheeks in his palm. She was so soft and delicate and all his.

"You never should've thought I was letting your ass move here without your man," he told her straight up.

She blushed. East was so protective and territorial, but in reality, that was how it was supposed to be. Your man should proudly claim you, and if he wasn't crazy about you and vice versa, then he was not the one, and you were not the one for him.

"I love you," Nia told East.

There was a time when they rarely mumbled those three special words, but lately, she couldn't stop professing her love for him. Every day he was pouring new vibes and energy into their pot of love, and she couldn't get enough of it.

"Love you more, boo," he told her, then smooched her lips.

East was happy that she had finally got that off her chest. He was tired of her keeping that one secret from him, even though he had already known about the move.

"Sooo . . ." She sighed.

East raised his eyebrow, wondering what else she had to confess. "More news?" he asked, probing.

She shook her head. "Nope. I'm feeling like Future right now, though," she said and hopped off his lap and began to do a li'l dance around the living room. Nia knew how much East enjoyed the rapper Future's music.

"How you feeling like that nigga?" he asked, confused.

She bopped her head to a beat that couldn't be heard.

"Now we got nine-oh-two-one-oh on our address," she said happily.

Nia was looking forward to making beautiful memories in a new city, business-wise and relationship-wise.

13

"I been living without limits. As far as my business, I'm the only one that's in control."

– Kanye West

Four months later . . .

"I have missed y'all so much. I really needed this," Nia confessed to her two best friends.

The trio was ducked off away from the paparazzi, the flashing lights, and the cameras in a booth in the back of STK, an American fine-dining restaurant in downtown L.A.

Nasi hugged her, since she and Nia were sitting right beside each other. "We've missed you more. The city ain't the same without you, baby love," she told her truthfully.

They all were busy. Nasi was planning her dream wedding, while Samone's business had taken off overnight, and Nia . . . Nia was being a modern-day Wonder Woman. She wasn't able to fly back and forth to New York as much as she had thought she would when she and East first moved to the West Coast. Business in L.A. was thriving, and she was so busy. Every day she was shaking hands with new contacts and sitting in the front row at fashion events and shows.

Nia loved the hustle and bustle of the city, and she felt like a newcomer all over again. Constantly, she was being inspired by the young, vibrant models. Even at night, while she lay in bed, with East by her side, she would get up and sketch a design that had randomly come to her mind. She was filling sketchbooks left and right and scanning the designs to her top seamstress back to New York. The L.A. boutique would be up and running in no time, and she was counting down until the grand opening.

"So, how are you and Mr. Sexy Face doing so far?" Nasi asked nosily.

Nia smiled and took a sip of her white wine before giving her friends the tea.

"Everything has been great. We are just struggling to get on the same page time-wise. Like, you know I'm an early bird, whereas he sleeps all day and is out all night. So, that's where the problems seem to come in at," she told them.

Samone asked, "And he's out doing what?"

Nia had never come out and told her friends that he was in the streets. She was sure they automatically assumed this.

"Handling his business, ma'am," she told Samone and stuck her tongue out playfully.

Nasi chimed in. "Hey, friend, I know you like 'em rough. I prefer 'em tall and pretty, though. Oh, and paid."

Samone laughed. "And I prefer them with a pussy some days and a dick other days." She rolled her eyes and tossed her hair over her shoulder.

"Oh, Lord, Mone! And, Nasi, my man is tall, sexy, and paid with a capital *P*," Nia told her friends.

They all shared another laugh, and then their faces lit up, because the food had finally arrived. They had been waiting almost an hour for dinner, but Nia had promised them that it was worth the wait.

"Are wedding bells in the forecast?" Samone asked Nia.

Nia damn near choked on the shrimp tempura. "Girl, don't kill me tonight, please," she begged after wiping her eyes and mouth.

"Marriage makes you wanna die? Damn, Nia. Tell us how you really feel," Nasi said.

Being the happy bride to be, they all expected Nasi to feel some type of way.

"Hey, I'm entitled to my opinion, boo. I am not ready for marriage right now. I am about to open another boutique. I bought that building up North, and then I have my workout line and lingerie too. No time for marriage," Nia explained to her friends.

"So, you're telling me that if he dropped on one knee right now, you would tell him no?" Nasi asked.

Nia was not running game on her. She knew her friend was in love.

She shook her head. "That's not what I'm saying. I would say yes and then tell him that we'll end up probably being engaged for about two years, because I'm too busy chasing my dreams right now to become someone's wife," she answered.

Samone nodded her head, totally understanding where she was coming from.

"So, what am I to you? A trophy wife in the making, because I'm not chasing my dreams right now?" Nasi asked. Her voice was full of attitude.

Nia turned in her seat and faced her. "Wait. When did this become about *you*? And did I call you a trophy wife?" she asked, not feeling the way Nasi was talking to her.

"I mean, that's what you basically said, Nia," Nasi said sarcastically.

Nia chuckled a little to keep from going the fuck off on her beloved friend. "Nasi, as I've told you, do you, boo. What you do and how you roll have no effect on me, and vice versa," she said.

Nia did not want to argue with her friends. When she'd asked them earlier in the week to come visit because she was in desperate need of girl talk and good company, she hadn't expected to have a heated conversation about *her* views on marriage.

"I don't appreciate how you look down on women who desire marriage. You don't have to give up on your dreams just because you're married," Nasi said.

Samone finally spoke up. "Says the girl who, as soon as she met Harry, stopped working," she said.

Nia took a deep breath. She knew things were about to go left.

"Bitch, what you say?" Nasi shouted.

Samone held her hands up and said, "Whoa now. Let's chill with the name-calling. We can have an adult conversation without calling names."

Nasi rolled her eyes and picked up her purse, which lay between Nia and herself. "I don't even know why I flew here. I had shit to do," she mumbled.

Samone retorted, "You came because our friend, who is always there for your drunk ass, needed us."

Nia sat back in her seat. She wanted nothing more than to return home and go to sleep at this point.

"Samone, fuck you. Nia, see you around. I'm catching a red-eye home," Nasi said before sliding out of the booth and disappearing into the crowded restaurant.

"That girl is crazy," Samone said and stuck her fork in Nasi's plate.

Nia agreed. "What happened that fast?" she asked.

Samone shrugged her shoulders. "Who knows? She was quiet on the flight, and then, when we got here, Harry wasn't answering the phone. So I don't think her issue is with us," she told Nia.

"I hope everything is okay," Nia told her.

Dinner was still pleasant, and Samone and Nia were able to catch up. Nia gave her friend a few business pointers as far as branding her business was concerned. They opted out of getting drinks and made plans to link up the next morning for brunch. After they left the restaurant, Nia stood on the sidewalk with Samone as they waited on her Uber to pull up.

"Okay, Mama. Call me when you make it in," Nia said when the Uber arrived. Nia kissed her friend's cheek. After Samone got in the car, Nia closed the car door, then walked across the street and hopped in East's Range Rover.

They had had his cars shipped here since he had spent so much money tricking them out, and he hadn't wanted to leave his cars at his house, unattended.

When she made it to the parking garage of the two-bedroom loft they were currently staying in while they resided in Los Angeles, Nia hopped out of the truck and grabbed the take-out plate she had brought home for East.

She was digging their new place, and it was safe to say East was too. It was important to her that she incorporated his personal style and taste into the loft's decor, since it was their first time living together officially. The walls were a mint-green color when they moved in, which went perfectly with the stained brown hardwood floors, and they had not changed the color.

The walls leading to the living-room area were covered in oversize photographs that Nia had taken herself. The best feature of the loft was the view overlooking the city. She hadn't overcrowded the living space with furniture. Only one couch was positioned in the middle of the floor in the living-room area, which also boasted an eighty-inch smart TV and a black mink rug.

The kitchen was small, which was okay, since it was only East and Nia. They mainly sat in the living room when they had dinner and watched a movie. The spare bedroom had been turned into a closet for both of them, since they both were shoe fanatics.

She loved their home, not because of the view or the comfortable bed that they had broken in during their first week in a new city, but because, together, the couple had made it *theirs*.

East's grandmother had flown out to help them get situated, since he hadn't wanted any of the movers Nia hired to touch his shit. Before she left, she had made a big spread of soul food and had prayed in the house, anointing their sacred places. She had left the couple with one gem. "Never go to bed angry with each other," she'd said, and so far, things had been going great between the two of them.

Or so Nia thought.

"Hey, babe. I'm home," Nia told East when she phoned him after she put his take-out plate in the refrigerator.

She was coming out of her shoes and clothes with every step she took. Two glasses of wine, Nasi storming out over some petty bullshit, and being stuck in traffic for almost an hour had Nia wanting only one thing right now, and that was her bed.

East was in the middle of something and couldn't really talk.

"All right, boo. Lock the door. You good?" he said, rushing the conversation.

She knew he was naturally paranoid from being in the streets most of his life, so she didn't protest when he insisted that they get an alarm installed at the loft. One of the main reasons Nia had chosen the particular building that they lived in was that it was gated and it had an around-the-clock security detail and private parking. In addition, each floor was assigned a specific key and code. It was impossible for a crazed person or a thief to get into the building.

"Yes. I'll be asleep when you get in," she told her boyfriend, and then she yawned loudly in his ear.

Of course, Nia telling him that she wouldn't be awake when he made it home piqued his interest.

"Nah. I'm about to come home, and I'll go back out when you fall asleep. We ain't having that," he told her, needing some love from his woman.

She giggled, knowing that he was going to say that, and that was exactly what she wanted. Today had been long, and her week had been even longer. The couple hadn't spent much time together, because their schedules kept conflicting. And normally, Fridays were their date nights, but her friends were in town.

"Okay, babe. See you when you get here," she told East as she rummaged through her lingerie drawer, looking for something enticing to put on for her man.

"I'll be there soon," he told her as he thumbed through a stack of cash.

East wanted to eyeball the amount, but he was fucking with the Underworld now, and that was a no-go.

"Okay, boo."

"Aye!" East called out to his girlfriend over the line.

Nia stopped looking at her figure in the oversize mirror that leaned against a wall in a corner of their bedroom. "Yes, love?" she said.

"You know how I want you when I come in, don't you?" he whispered, not wanting anyone to hear him.

Her pussy jumped as she thought about what would go down as soon as Daddy made it home.

"Yes," she answered.

"How, babe?" East asked, to be sure.

She bit down on her bottom lip.

With her eyes closed, she tugged on one of her nipples and said, "Face down, ass up."

***

"Turn around . . . to the left, sweetheart," Nia instructed the model, whom she had standing at the edge of the runway.

Nia stood back and crossed her arms as she carefully studied the look. Preparing for a fashion show took a lot of effort and time. Not only did the music have to be perfect, but so did the lights and the stage layout. As far as the fashion concept of the show, that was a serious matter to Nia. Careful consideration and tons of thought went into planning all aspects of her shows, which was why she rarely had her own fashion shows.

Nia Hudson presenting a new line was a big-ass, fucking deal. She had reached a point in her career where it was rare that her designs graced the runway. Her favorite thing to do now was help new designers plan their shows.

The lingerie line that she had been diligently crafting and preparing for would be launching soon, and because she wasn't a last-minute person, Nia had the models prepping now.

"I don't like this look on her. Go get the, um . . . It's a black sheer nightie with a fur-collar robe. Go get that. Let's see that on her," Nia told one of the interns.

She told the model, "Take that off."

The color in the model's face drained out. "Right here?" she asked.

Nia turned around and faced her. "Is there a problem?" she questioned.

"Can I go in the back and change?" She was too ashamed to change in front of a room full of people.

"If you want. It's quicker to change right here, though. I have about forty-two models to go through," Nia said.

The model dropped her head. "Please."

Nia hopped on the runway and got in the model's personal space. She pulled off the BOY skully that she wore low on her head. "Do you see this scar?" she asked the model.

No one had really ever got a good look at the scar. If Nia didn't concealed the scar with her hair, then she covered it with concealer and foundation.

The young woman nodded her head. She had never been this close to anyone famous, and she felt like, at any moment, she would faint.

"My ex-boyfriend threw a lamp at me because he thought I was cheating on him. I have hated this scar my whole life, but guess what? I don't care anymore," Nia revealed, confiding in the girl.

Although the room was full of people working, some of the models sat on the floor, waiting on their name or number to be called. Everyone's eyes were now on Nia Hudson and the model whom no one knew.

The model wasn't famous, and it was her first show. Nia had found the chick on Instagram and had personally DM'd her, asking her to fly to Los Angeles to be in her fashion show.

Nia thought she was beautiful, with her doe-shaped eyes, dark and creamy chocolate skin, and her thighs. . . . Oh, Nia had stared at her hips and thighs in all her pictures. The girl was the perfect height and shape, and when Nia closed her eyes and envisioned women of all shapes, sizes, colors, figures, and races, she was who came to mind.

If the girl didn't possess sassiness and confidence, how could she slay the runway at a fashion show showcasing lingerie?

"I need you to tap into whatever you need to, to turn on your bad bitch. We all got it in us," Nia told her.

The model nodded her head. She understood what Nia was saying. She flashed her a smile and hopped off the runway.

"Kate, take her to the back so she can get dressed," Nia told her assistant. "Next!" she called, instructing the next model to come out.

Thirteen hours later, Nia was still working. She had come out of her tennis shoes and was now walking around the room in a pair of fuzzy socks. Her hair was pulled back into a bun, and her glasses sat on the tip of her nose.

If she wasn't coaching the models on how to walk, she was helping the seamstresses make alterations on the lingerie pieces. Then she would saunter over to the technical crew to give her opinion on the lights and the background display.

"Where are we now?" Nia asked Kate, who was responsible for overseeing the invite list.

"Everyone has confirmed, for the most part. Your friend Nasi opened the e-mail, but she didn't respond," Kate told her.

Nia rolled her eyes. "Girl, I'll handle that. Let's get a budget over to Peter by tomorrow."

Both of Nia's phones were dead, so she asked Kate, "Can I use your phone to call my boyfriend?"

Kate handed her an iPhone. "And I ordered food for everyone. We have been here since this—"

Nia waved her hand, cutting her off. "That's cool," she told her and walked away. She often forgot that not everyone was like her. Whenever she was in the zone, food was the last thing on her mind.

"Bae, my phone's dead," Nia told East as soon as he answered.

He huffed, "I been calling you all day, Ma."

She detected the attitude in his voice. "I'm sorry. It has been crazy around here. I'm so glad Kate flew in to help me," she told him.

East had just filled his gas tank, and now he placed the gas nozzle back in the holder and finished up with his car so he could get in and focus on the conversation with his girl.

"You tired? Have you eaten?" he asked, concerned about Nia, as he climbed behind the wheel.

She had been working like a slave for the past two weeks and was up and out the door before he could roll over and hold on to her waist in his sleep. The last two times he brought up taking a vacation, she had brushed him off, so East had decided to let it go for now.

"Kate ordered for everyone," she told him.

"Okay, but are you going to eat?" he asked, knowing that she probably wasn't going to touch the food.

Nia was too busy watching one of the models try to squeeze into a onesie and didn't hear East's question. "You can't fit into that," she yelled as she marched in the girl's direction.

"Babe, let me call you back," Nia said into the phone before hanging up.

East could only shake his head at Nia. She had turned into a diva, but that was how she was when her money was on the line. She had invested her own funds in the lingerie line and had been on pins and needles ever since. She'd stepped out on faith when it came to her new business ventures because she didn't want to have too many stakeholders in her company.

Faith was one of the most important things that a business owner needed to have. It was the evidence of things unseen and unheard, and if anyone knew about making a way out of no way, it was Nia Hudson. From the projects to the top floor in a million-dollar building, if that wasn't faith, then she didn't know what was.

The night went on, and Nia was on her umpteenth cup of coffee. The models were beginning to look like walking zombies, and Nia hadn't even noticed. The show was in six weeks, and in her opinion, they had a long way to go and a lot of work to do.

Kate took a deep breath before knocking on the door to the small storage closet that Nia had turned into her office.

"Yeah?" she called out. Her face was buried in a stack of magazines. She wanted to bring in about seven more models, a few chicks who stood taller than six feet.

"Nia, is it okay if the models go home?" Kate asked.

Many of them were unaware of how hard Nia Hudson worked, but Kate was very familiar with her workaholism and shared it. In fact, it was one of the reasons why Kate had climbed the company ladder and was now Nia's right-hand girl. Kate was persistent, determined, and dedicated, and for her diligence, she had been rewarded.

Nia had bought her a 2015 Mercedes-Benz coupe, had paid off her student loans, and paid her rent and other bills on a monthly basis. She didn't do that for show, and Nia had told Kate that what she did for her and her family or how much she compensated Kate for her services was no one's business.

There weren't too many assistants bringing in one hundred fifty thousand dollars a year and receiving a shopping stipend, but Kate did. Nia knew that half of the things she'd accomplished in the past year wouldn't have been possible if Kate hadn't been rocking with her during those late nights and early mornings at the design studio.

Nia snatched her glasses off and asked Kate, "Did they say they wanted to leave?"

She shook her head. "No, but they look so tired, and they're just sitting around."

Nia stood to her feet, grabbed her iPad, and passed Kate, then walked down the hallway to the back of the large space that she had rented for rehearsals. She hadn't yet decided where the fashion show would be.

"You all can leave if you want to," she said when she reached the models.

It was a test, and many of them would fail. She knew it.

She took a seat at the edge of the runway, with her iPad in hand, and pretended to be busy, when in fact she was only scrolling through her timeline, since she hadn't been on social media in a few days.

Many of the models grunted in satisfaction over finally being dismissed. Some of them ran out, while others were so sore from prancing around in heels all day that they moseyed out the door.

About fifteen minutes later, Nia looked up and saw that only six models remained on the floor.

"Y'all not leaving?" she asked those models, to be sure.

There were a few other models that had not yet made it all the way out the door. They looked at each other, not knowing what to say.

"Do y'all wanna leave?" she asked the departing models.

One of them spoke up. "No."

A wide smile swept across Nia's face. "Good. Let's get to work," she told that one model at the door and the six others on the floor.

Nia fanned the other models out the door. "Oh no. Y'all were tired, remember? Good-bye," she said. And then she told the seven remaining girls to follow her.

Two hours later, she had been able to spend one-on-one time with the models and had been able to get honest feedback about the line. She was impressed with the small group. She had had each of them walk the runway a few times, and they had critiqued each other. Nia had even taken a few selfies with the models and had posted on her social media accounts, with the caption Late-night grinding with a few pretty girls.

"Kate, let's make sure these ladies get a good night's rest. We will be going to London in few days," Nia said and stood to her feet, prepared to go home.

The time on her Rolex watch read 4:53 a.m., and she needed rest.

"London?" asked the girl from Instagram, not believing she'd heard her correctly.

Nia smiled and nodded her head. "Yeah, I want you all to see a fashion show from the front row. Hopefully, it helps you ladies prepare for how it's going to be when it's y'all on that runway," she told them.

Screams, clapping, and shrieks could be heard as Nia took the side door out of the building and hopped in her truck.

Kate immediately texted her, You rock.

She sent Kate instructions to make sure everyone had a passport and to see about renting a house for the girls while they were in London. God had blessed her, and she had made it her personal goal in life to give back as much as she could.

She headed home.

"Can we get one more bottle of this wine?" Nia asked the server.

East raised an eyebrow. "One more bottle?" he teased his girlfriend.

Her shoulders dropped, and she tossed back the last gulp of her wine. "Babe, I so needed this tonight. You're the best," she told him, tipsy.

"You been grinding, Ma," he commented.

If Nia wasn't with the models at the warehouse, then she was over on Rodeo Drive, overseeing the renovations on the boutique. On Friday nights she would fly to New York to be at the boutique on Saturday morning, and then she would fly back to L.A. later that night and would cook dinner on Sundays. She was trying to do it all, and so far, she had been successful. She was tired, but it didn't matter.

Nia had started the year with several goals in mind, and so far, everything was flowing, and she prayed it stayed that way.

"You have too," she told him.

They had not spent much time together lately, and when she'd come home tonight, she discovered that he had left simple instructions for her to look her best. He would be there to pick her up at 9:00 p.m. sharp.

It had been so long since they went out on the town and acted like a couple, and tonight was necessary. As always, East was right on time with his romantic gestures.

He'd walked into their loft, with one single red rose and a small gift bag with a silver Cartier bracelet, and it had brought Nia to tears.

Now, as they sat across from each other at dinner, she couldn't stop praising him and showering him with her love and affection.

"Yeah, I love it out here, no lie," he admitted.

Business was booming, and the Underworld was a completely different ball game. The one thing that he loved so far about the new organization was that he was a part of the security. East went to bed with less stress and fewer concerns on his mind. No longer did he feel the need to look over his shoulder every two seconds.

His cousin, Papa, had told him that he was not untouchable. Although bullets never had names on them and could hit whoever the target was, Papa had also assured him that no one would want to fuck with him.

Not even Harlem, East's best friend.

He and Harlem had not had a sit-down yet, because Nia had needed to move ASAP, so there was no going-away celebration or dinner. They had moved in silence.

Harlem had been calling and texting East, wondering what was up. He had heard a few things through the grapevine, but until the words came out of East's mouth and East told him that he had switched over and joined the other side, Harlem wouldn't react the way he wanted to.

"Me too," Nia told him, loving that they were on the same page.

After dinner, they went bowling and then to a bar that Nia wanted to check out.

"Okay, no more for you." East took the third shot glass away from Nia after she downed yet another drink.

She pretended to pout. "I thought you liked me better when I was drunk?"

"I love you however you are, but I'm not about to be carrying you in the house. I went to the gym this morning. I'm sore," he admitted.

Nia rolled her eyes. "Oh, whatever."

Her song came over the speakers, and she lifted her hands in the air and twirled around in a circle. East couldn't do anything but laugh and cheer her on. She appeared to be happy and carefree. It had been a few weeks since he and Nia hung out, and he knew tonight was the first time she was not thinking about her upcoming fashion show.

"You see it moving, don't you?" Nia asked East, in reference to the fact that she was making her ass cheeks move one at a time.

He pulled her closer and kissed her neck. "Cut that out," he teased.

"This your ass, ain't it, baby?" she asked.

With pleasure, she was all his and would be his forever.

"Yep." He smacked her ass and gripped her butt cheek, not caring that other patrons in the bar were looking over at them as they acted like drunk lovers.

Nia slid her tongue into his mouth and kissed him passionately. East sucked on her tongue, causing her to moan lightly.

"Mmm." East turned around and ordered Nia another shot.

"I thought I couldn't have anymore, baby?" she said playfully, knowing what he was trying to do.

"You're with me, so you are good. Drink up," he told her. When her shot arrived, he tossed one back with her.

The burning sensation in her chest didn't bother her now, but the shots paired with the wine she had had at the restaurant meant that Nia would regret overindulging in alcohol when she woke up in the morning.

"Whew," she exclaimed as she slammed the shot glass on the bar top.

East bobbed his head to the beat. The bar had a nice vibe. He scoped out the scene and made a mental note to hit Papa up on a business tip. East wanted to open up a few businesses, and he would love to see one of these bars in the hood.

"What you looking at?" Nia asked him.

East told her, "I like it in here."

She nodded her head. "Me too," she agreed. "And they drinks cheap."

He laughed at how cheap she was when it came to anything that wasn't clothes or shoes. When they shopped, he hardly saw her take a peek at a price tag.

"Ooh! This is my song!" she exclaimed.

Nia wrapped her hands around her hips. With her eyes closed, she moved to the beat, and East pulled her to him, not wanting anyone to bump into her at the crowded bar, because then he would have to beat somebody's ass.

"Oh, baby, drunk in love we be all night," she sang in his ear.

14

"To be honest, dawg, I ain't feelin' your energy."

– Kanye West

"Pinkie promise me you'll be back in time."

As stood on the sidewalk at the airport, Nia held on to her man's waist, not wanting him to leave her, but business had called him back home, and East had no choice but to dip.

He kissed her once more and promised her for the millionth time in the past hour. "I'll be there, babe," he said.

Nia sighed and hugged him tighter. East was making her soft. She had never thought the day would come when she would be damn near on the verge of tears over the prospect of spending a few days without her beau. She was heartbroken. She was already dreading going home.

"Cheer up. You been busy, anyway," he told her.

She didn't argue with him there. PURE, her lingerie line, was being launched in the next seventy-two hours. Nia had been a wreck for the past few weeks. She and East hadn't spent much time together and had barely communicated via text message and over the phone.

As soon as she would walk through the front door of their home, Nia would force herself to eat a sandwich or a piece of fruit before showering and falling asleep on the couch. East would come home hours later and put her in the bed, praying that once the lingerie line was up and in stores, she would allow him to whisk her away on vacation.

Nia had lost so much weight in the past few weeks, and she was running on zero energy on a daily basis. She knew the sacrifices that needed to be made in order to ensure that the fashion show was a success. Years had passed since the time when she first entered the game. This was nothing new to her, but it was to East, and he didn't like how skinny she was getting.

In Nia's mind, sleep was for dreamers. She was no longer dreaming. Her days were now filled with fulfillment, fulfilling her dreams and making them her reality.

The grind had definitely been real, and in three days, once the curtains were pulled back and the lights went low, it would all be worth it.

The who's who in the fashion industry had been invited to the show. Even the haters and critics had been extended an invitation. Nia didn't like yes-men around her, which was why she had given the tough critics and fashion designers front-row seats and her close friends the second row. Nia wasn't looking for or expecting praise and a standing ovation. She preferred the honest truth.

"I love you," Nia told East. She handed him his phone. "Scan this," she instructed.

"I've flown a million times, boo," he reminded her and kissed her forehead.

He loved to see her smitten with him. He waited patiently on these days.

"I know, I know. I just don't want you to leave," she said, pouting.

Time was flying, and if East wanted to make his flight, it was best that he told Nia good-bye and walked into the airport. She slid her shades back on her face and stepped back so he could pick up his luggage.

"I'm going to hit you when I land," he told her.

"Okay."

East lifted her head up by her chin and bent down and kissed her lips. "Keep it tight for me," he teased, and then he walked off before they started another conversation.

Nia sighed and leaned against the truck as she watched her beau walk into the airport.

Damn. I am going to miss Daddy, she thought to herself as she got back into the Range Rover.

Minutes later, she headed back to the venue that she had chosen for the fashion show. As soon as she walked into the place, she saw that it was a madhouse, but the crazy thing was that it ignited something in the pit of Nia's gut. Everyone running around "like chickens with their heads cut off" caused her to smile. She was happy *and* anxious about the show.

Men were toting large plants. Kate had two phones to her ears and a clipboard full of notes. The models were practicing on the runway, while seamstresses were making sure measurements were perfect.

Nia took a seat on the last row and closed her eyes. As loud as it was around her, she heard nothing but the sound of a money counter.

PURE was brilliant. The pieces were sexy yet affordable. She had designed pieces for the Coke-bottle figure and the A-cup woman who wished she had double DDs when she was prancing around the house for her man. Nia had lingerie sets for the curvy sisters, and she even had a few outfits for the grandma who wanted to get her groove back. She had made sure that every woman would be represented at the fashion show.

Several deals were on the table for the lingerie line, but Nia was allowing her finance department to handle negotiations. As long as she made her money back and turned a healthy profit, she was good to go.

"Nia, are you okay? Do you need something?" Kate asked after she noticed her boss was sitting there and not doing anything, which wasn't like Nia Hudson.

The definitions of *hardworking*, *determined*, and *ambitious* all had Nia's picture under them. She was much like a modern-day Wonder Woman, but with an *N* on her chest.

"No, I'm good. Let's do a run-through of the show. I want to see it from back here," she told Kate.

Nia pulled her cell phone out of her pocket and laid it on the seat next to her. She stretched her legs and then crossed her arms, preparing to be wowed. She had handpicked each and every one of the models, and individually, they brought something sexy to the runway when they graced it.

"Will do," Kate said and then walked off to call all the models to the back for yet another run-through.

Nia was on pins and needles. A glass of wine would have calmed her nerves, but she did not want to have alcohol on her breath when she talked to the press. Reporters were good for spinning a story. She could see the headlines now, DESIGNER NIA HUDSON DRUNK AT HER OWN SHOW.

She sat in a director's chair, in a pink silk robe, tapping her feet against the footrest as the makeup artist touched up her makeup. Nia didn't sweat often, but for some reason, she could not stop perspiring. Her eyeliner kept running down her face, and her foundation was beginning to appear smudgy.

"Kate, is the music ready to go? How is the green room looking? Did Samone and Nasi arrive yet?" Nia asked. She had been asked her assistant a million questions for the past three hours.

Kate nodded her head to every question as Nia asked it. "Yes, ma'am. Are you dressed? *Entertainment Tonight* is ready to interview you."

Nia told her she needed her shoes, and then she would be ready to go.

After getting her makeup touched up for the third time tonight, Nia snuck into the private room reserved for her and slipped off the robe. She sprayed her body with perfume and fluffed out her Marilyn Monroe–inspired curls and made sure the screws in her earrings were tight.

That morning, East had had roses and a pair of diamond earrings hand delivered to the venue, with a note promising to be at the show tonight, rooting his lady on.

Nia prayed that he kept good on his promise, because she missed him so much and wanted nothing more than to be wrapped up in his arms once the madness died down. For the past few weeks, the fashion show had been her entire life. Everything had been put on the back burner, including overseeing the renovations on the L.A. boutique and speaking engagements.

Nia had been eating, sleeping, and breathing PURE. If reporters caught her out, and she actually gave them a few minutes of her time, the only thing she would mumble was, "PURE." Pure was her baby, and in an hour, it would be birthed, for all the world to see.

She called East again, only for the call to go to voice mail. Nia sighed and tossed the phone into her garment bag and went to promote her brand before the show started.

Nia answered as many questions from the press as she could before the show director came and told her that they needed to start ASAP if they wanted to remain on schedule and avoid a fine for staying past the permitted time.

As they walked to their seats in the front row, Samone asked Nia, "Where is East?"

"Same thing I want to know," she told her best friend, wishing her boyfriend and number one supporter were sitting next to her.

Samone and Nasi, whom Nia had spoken with earlier that day, had always been on the left and right side of her at all her shows, but she had been looking forward to finally having the one she spent the most time with holding her hand.

East knew the ins and outs of putting PURE together, and even though this was her business, her brand, her vision, and her ideas coming to life, this was a moment that she really wanted to share with him. She took her seat, waved, and spoke to a few of her associates in the fashion industry before she got comfortable, crossing one long leg over the other.

The show came to life in a matter of seconds.

Five, four, three, two, one . . . , she thought, her tension rising.

After the third model came out and killed the runway, Nia began to relax, knowing that tonight would be a success. The models were fierce. Their makeup was on fleek, their hair was laid, and the lingerie was hot. There was nothing in the stores that resembled Nia's designs.

A tap on Nia's shoulder caused her to turn around, and she found Demi bending down in the second row.

Nia smiled and whispered, "Hey. Y'all made it. Where is Papa? Did my assistant not send you the message about where your seats would be?"

Demi hated that she couldn't return Nia's warm smile. "I think you need to come with me," she said.

In that moment, Nia knew something had happened. . . .

Part II
Coming Soon